PENGUIN BOOKS

the bodysurfers

Robert Drewe was born in Melbourne and grew up
on the West Australian coast. His novels and short
stories have been widely translated, won many
national and international prizes, and been adapted
for film, television, radio and the theatre. He has
also written plays, screenplays, journalism and film
criticism, and edited two international anthologies
of stories. He lives with his family in Sydney.

ROBERT DREWE

the bodysurfers

PENGUIN BOOKS

Penguin Books Australia Ltd
487 Maroondah Highway, PO Box 257
Ringwood, Victoria 3134, Australia
Penguin Books Ltd
Harmondsworth, Middlesex, England
Penguin Putnam Inc.
375 Hudson Street, New York, New York 10014, USA
Penguin Books Canada Limited
10 Alcorn Avenue, Toronto, Ontario, Canada M4V 3B2
Penguin Books (NZ) Ltd
Cnr Rosedale and Airborne Roads, Albany, Auckland, New Zealand
Penguin Books (South Africa) (Pty) Ltd
5 Watkins Street, Denver Ext 4, 2094, South Africa
Penguin Books India (P) Ltd
11, Community Centre, Panchsheel Park, New Delhi 110 017, India

First published by James Fraser Publishing Pty Ltd 1983
Published by Pan Macmillan Australia Pty Ltd 1987
This edition published by Penguin Books Australia Ltd 2001
Offset from the Picador edition

1 3 5 7 9 10 8 6 4 2

Copyright © Robert Drewe 1983

The moral right of the author has been asserted

All rights reserved. Without limiting the rights under copyright reserved above,
no part of this publication may be reproduced, stored in or introduced into a retrieval
system, or transmitted, in any form or by any means (electronic, mechanical,
photocopying, recording or otherwise), without the prior written permission
of both the copyright owner and the above publisher of this book.

Cover design and digital imaging by Ellie Exarchos
Cover images by Getty Images and photolibrary.com
Printed and bound in Australia by McPherson's Printing Group, Maryborough, Victoria

National Library of Australia
Cataloguing-in-Publication data:

Drewe, Robert, 1943– .
The bodysurfers.

ISBN 0 14 100801 6.

I. Title.

A823.3

www.penguin.com.au

Just as Samson after being shorn of his hair was left eyeless in Gaza, was this generation, stripped bare of all faith, to be left comfortless on Bondi Beach?

Manning Clark

Lying —
side by side —
we heard the rising ocean
to the dying wind replying,
heard its surge advance with still insistent call
or subside
to the night-wind's dying fall

Christopher Brennan

We'll pick up the bikini girls as soon as they take off their beach wraps, and we'll have their beach wraps back on them before the boys can let out a single *hubba-hubba*.

Bill 'The Whale' Willis, the beach inspector
who arrested the first bikini girl at Bondi

To Candida

Contents

The Manageress and the Mirage

M y father wasn't in his element in party hats. His head was too big; the mauve crêpe-paper crown stretched around his wide forehead looked neither festive nor humorous, just faintly ridiculous. Annie and David and I sat embarrassed in silly hats as well. They were compulsory fun, Dad was definite about them. We'd always worn them at home and the normal Christmas dinner routine was being followed wherever possible.

There was one major difference this Christmas: because our mother had died in July we were having dinner at the Seaview Hotel instead of at home. Consequently we were observing several other minor variations on our traditional dinner — we ate roast turkey instead of the usual chicken and ham, we children were allowed glasses of pink champagne alongside our glasses of lemonade, and the plum pudding contained plastic tokens like Monopoly symbols — obviously poked into the pudding later — rather than real threepences and sixpences cooked into it.

When Dad suggested that we eat dinner at the hotel we agreed readily enough. Since July we'd had a middle-aged woman, Gladys Barker, housekeeping for us. Dad called her Glad to her face, but to us he sometimes called her Gladly — as in the hymn 'Gladly My Cross I'd Bear' — because of her sighs around the house and air of constant martyrdom. We thought this was funny, but at the time we thought he was saying 'Gladly, My Cross-Eyed Bear' so we had it wrong for five or six years. Glad's cooking was unexceptional, a depressing prospect for Christmas dinner, and anyway, without anyone spelling it out, this Christmas we wanted to keep the family unit tight and self-contained.

I caught Annie's and David's eyes from time to time, but they showed only a vague self-consciousness as we sat in the hotel dining room in our party hats and school uniforms, picking at our meals, gingerly sipping pink champagne and pulling crackers. Dad was becoming increasingly amiable, however, even hearty. It was clear to us that he was making an effort. He made jokes and we laughed at them, for him rather than with him, out of mutual support.

'Remember I was travelling the other week to a sales conference down at Albany?' he said. 'Well, I stopped overnight at Mount Barker. I went down to dinner in the hotel dining room and on the menu was rabbit casserole. I said to the waitress, "Excuse me, dear, is that with or without myxomatosis?"'

'"I wouldn't know," she said, very po-faced, "It's all in the gravy."'

He was trying hard for all our sakes. It had not dawned on me before that I loved him and the realisation was slightly embarrassing.

Soon he became the dining room's focus of attention. Selecting a plastic whistle from the cracker debris, he blew it gamely. Other nearby guests, observing us and seeing the lie of the land, smiled encouragingly at us and followed suit. An old fellow gave Annie his cracker toy. A fat man tickled his wife's nose with a feathered whistle; she balanced a champagne cork on his sunburnt head. Crackers popped and horns tooted. Above these antics a fan slowly revolved.

Beyond the high expanse of windows the ocean glistened into the west, where atmospheric conditions had magically turned Rottnest Island into three distinct islands. Annie was struck by the mysterious asymmetry of this illusion.

'It's gone wrong,' she said loudly, pointing out to sea. The other guests began murmuring about the phenomenon. Annie's plaits looked irregular; one was thicker than the other; Dad still hadn't mastered them. 'The lighthouse has gone,' she said.

'No, it's still there,' Dad said, and tried to explain mirages, mentioning deserts and oases, with emphasis on the Sahara. I knew the horizon was always twelve miles away, but I couldn't grasp the idea of shifting islands or the creation of non-existent ones. So thirsty people in deserts saw visions of water — why would people bursting with food and drink see visions of land?

As our plates were being removed our table drew special attention from the hotel manageress. A handsome dark-haired woman in her thirties, she clapped her hands authoritatively for more champagne, and more crackers for us to pull, and joined us for a drink, inquiring about our presents with oddly curious eyes. Dad introduced us.

She announced to me, 'You do look like your father, Max.' She remarked on Annie's pretty hair and on the importance of David looking after his new watch. Sportively, she donned a blue paper crown and looked at us over the rim of her champagne glass. As the plum pudding was being served she left the table and returned with gifts for us wrapped in gold paper — fountain pens for David and me, a doll for Annie. Surprised, we looked to Dad for confirmation.

He showed little surprise at the gifts, however, only polite gratitude, entoning several times, 'Very, very kind of you.'

'Rex, it gave me pleasure,' the manageress said. 'They're a credit to you.' She called him Rex, not Mr Lang. His eyes were moist at her compliment. He lit a cigar and leaned back in his seat, crown askew, like Old King Cole.

After the plum pudding (he and the manageress had brandies

instead) and another cracker pulling we thanked her again for our presents, on his instructions, and he sent us outside while he paid the bill.

'Get some fresh air, kids,' he said.

We trooped out to the car park. Before today the car park had been the only part of the Seaview Hotel familiar to us. Sometimes on Saturday mornings we'd languished there, watching the ocean swells roll in, dying for a swim, squabbling in the Ford's back seat or desultorily reading Shell road maps from the glovebox while Dad had a drink or two.

'I have to see a chap about something,' he'd say, bringing us out glasses of raspberry lemonade. A frightening hubbub sounded from the bar, yet he would turn and stride back into this noise and smoke and beer-smell with all the cheer in the world.

Outside, the mirage persisted. Rottnest was still three oddly attenuated islands which seemed to be sailing south. The afternoon sea breeze was late and the temperature lingered in the nineties. The heat haze smudged the definition of the horizon and the Indian Ocean stretched flat and slick to Mauritius and beyond before curving into the sky.

David said, 'Did you smell her perfume?' and made a face. He loosened his tie and farted from the champagne. Annie poked at her doll's eyes. 'I've got one like this called Amanda,' she said. We presumed who had given her the other doll yet by unspoken agreement no one mentioned her. I knew the others were thinking that normally at this time we'd be unwrapping presents from the tree. She would play cheery Christmas records on the radiogram and run from the kitchen bringing us mints and nuts and little mince pies.

Eyes remained dry as we walked to the car. The car park was almost empty because of the bars being closed for Christmas. Asphalt bubbled, a broken beer glass from Christmas Eve sat on

13

the verandah rail and the smell of stale beer settled over the beer garden. Around the garden's dusty, worn lawn, red and yellow hibiscuses wilted in the heat. Christmas was running short of breath. One after another, David, Annie and I snatched off our party hats, crumpled them and threw them on the ground.

The imaginary islands, showing smoky silhouettes of hills and tall trees, kept sailing south. From the car you could see into the manageress's office. She was combing his hair where his party hat had ruffled it. He came out whistling 'Jingle Bells' and the stench of his cigar filled the car.

The Silver Medallist

It was possibly lucky my mother didn't marry her first fiancé because he ended up in Fremantle Prison. For a while as a youth he was a local hero and then his life tailed off and began deteriorating rapidly shortly after I knew him.

Older sports fans might remember the name Kevin Parnell. Competing with severe influenza, he nevertheless won a silver medal for the 800 metres freestyle at the Berlin Olympics. There were plenty of snapshots of him in the old photograph albums Annie constantly pored over as a girl. In those days, when she was in trouble with Dad — and even after she realised she was thereby negating her own existence — she used to dramatically wish aloud that Mum had married Kevin instead. She would point out airily that he was more handsome than Dad, which was true, and, because the album photographs all showed him frolicking in the water, acrobatically skylarking about as the centre-man in a human pyramid of brown and toothy young beachgoers, or clowning in fancy dress at the surf club ball, obviously more fun than our bad-tempered father as well. (This last assumption was wrong, or must have been in 1940 when Rex Lang appeared on the scene and, with little apparent advantage other than a perceptible twinkle in the eye, swept Joan Crossing out of the ex-Olympian's muscular arms.)

When I first met Kevin Parnell he was about forty. He knew I was Joan's son but he never mentioned her to me, not even to mutter that he was sorry to hear of her death, and I certainly didn't bring the subject up. He was a top swimming coach at Crawley Baths and he had another business on Cottesloe Beach hiring out rubber surf shooters and selling sun bathers a coating of suntan oil. He was tall and getting fleshy by then, with a thick smooth chest and wavy black hair that put you in mind of those old Charles Atlas advertisements. Twenty years after his competition days he still carried himself with an Olympian's elan, whether shouting instructions at 6.00 a.m. to his shivering squad of teenage swimmers, of which I was one, or presiding over his beach shelter, and the beach, four hours later.

It was at the beach, before the general public, that he allowed the 'character' side of his personality full sway. On the beach he always wore a straw hat with a red band and a brief pair of leopard print trunks. His red and white striped shelter carried a big sign with a picture of a mutton bird on it and the slogan *Kevin Parnell — The World Famous Suntan Champion.* On the outside walls hung old press pictures of his swimming victories and others of him spraying Bob Hope's shoulders with oil, mock-sparring with Rocky Marciano and shaking hands with ex-King Peter of Yugoslavia (in a double-breasted lounge suit), all encased in protective smeary plastic and, in the case of the celebrity shots, all taken more or less where you stood at that moment. The oil he sprayed on his customers was derived from the oil glands of mutton birds hunted in the islands of Bass Strait by the descendants of nineteenth-century sailors and the Tasmanian Aboriginal women they had kidnapped. He had a slightly smaller sign proclaiming himself *The Mutton Bird King.*

From us hanging around the beach one summer holiday, Annie became friendly with Parnell's daughter, Geraldine. I would have liked to — she was pretty, dark-haired and long-limbed, with high, full breasts — but she was distant with me, not exactly standoffish, more as if she saw me only indistinctly. She helped her father with the spraying and shooter hiring, working away in her bikini while we boys admired her even more for her indifference.

Annie said Geraldine was really a lonely girl. Her mother had died young, too. I thought this may have been link between them, that and Annie's old curiosity about Kevin Parnell. I'm sure that in a way she saw Geraldine as a permutation of herself — how she might have turned out if Parnell had married our mother; if he had been her father.

Parnell gave the impression he was king of the beach as well as of the mutton birds. He was what used to be known as 'a man's man', meaning that he was a hearty male chauvinist with a gregarious manner which always attracted a knot of off-duty newspaper reporters, university students, lifesavers and other beach types who flocked into the bar of the local hotel. Each day at twelve he'd set off for a drink, saying, 'The sun's over the yardarm!' and leaving Geraldine to look after business. At two o'clock, chuckling, straw hat rakish, stomach gleaming, he'd saunter back to the beach, pausing for a quip or two with some sunbaking woman on the way.

After his lunchtime beers he usually made a show of having a swim before returning to work. We got to know his routine. He'd skim his hat at a likely looking girl, calling, 'Look after this, darling,' hitch up his trunks, rub his hands together so his shoulder muscles moved around, and then race down to the ocean, scattering sand, and dive with a belly-whacking thump into the waves.

He would rise slowly to the surface snorting like a buffalo, throw his hair back into place, and then strike out for the surf-race marker buoy, three hundred yards out to sea. This performance wasn't wasted. He still had his old deceptively languid swimming style. We'd notice women's eyes following him around the buoy, turning towards the beach, sprinting to catch a wave and riding triumphantly in, head down, shoulders hunched, one leg bent up behind him in the Hawaiian manner. Towards the end of the ride, before the wave lost power, he'd somersault out of it and come to an abrupt stop. (I imagined silent cheers in a hundred throats.) He would spring to his feet, clear his nose, bang the water from his ears, smooth back his hair and, smiling benignly, retrieve his hat and stride majestically back to the shelter.

The Saturday afternoon which seemed to set various events in motion I was lounging self-consciously on a deck chair in the shade of the Parnell's awning trying to simultaneously develop a conversation with Geraldine as she worked, appear publicly relaxed and surreptitiously covet her body. It was about 2.30, and ninety degrees Fahrenheit. There was a sting in the sun and business was brisk. The air was thick and sweet with oil and her skin gleamed where the mist had settled on her. I noted the white shaved skin of her armpit glistening as she raised the spraygun to squirt her taller clients' shoulders and I also noticed that most males tried to look down her bikini top when she bent to spray their legs.

Her father returned from the pub with a bigger entourage than usual that afternoon. I heard him running across the car park, laughing and grunting as the bitumen burnt his feet, and then thudding down the wooden ramp to the beach. Some lifesavers and a couple of girls were with him. The men were strangers, with the names of famous far-off surf clubs on their T-shirts, visiting for the surf championships that weekend. They were all merry and boisterous. Parnell was in his element. The visitors were his types. They bantered and teased but they also observed a deference to him that he liked. Of course they were delighted to meet Geraldine, even sobered for a moment at first sight of her. I saw she was taken aback by them and by their status, especially by a fair-headed fellow who, in the way of these matters, assumed and was granted by his companions some sort of priority in flirting with her. I was introduced in a perfunctory way ('This is young David Lang over here'), but by the time the fair-headed one had asked her to spray him I'd had enough and I sloped off.

I skirted around the visitors for the next hour or so. They were much in evidence on the beach, ostentatiously bodysurfing, vigorously passing a football back and forth on the sand, Rugby-style, and generally creating a rowdy athletic presence. I was about to leave when I saw a small crowd of beachgoers gathering halfway along the beach. They were all looking at a black swan, surrounding it in a vaguely curious way as if to see what it would do next. The swan was bedraggled and looked far from home.

It was definitely out of sorts, squatting disconsolately on the sand, hissing softly and occasionally raising and lowering a dishevelled wing. Two children threw sand at it tentatively and a yellow Labrador barked gingerly in its general direction.

It wasn't long before Parnell saw the crowd and came down through the sand to investigate. Geraldine and a couple of the lifesavers were with him. He immediately assumed control of the situation. You could almost hear his brain ticking over: this is a water-bird and there is the water; it must be returned to it at once.

He scooped up the surprised swan, held it to his chest with one arm, walked into the ocean and began side-stroking out to sea. Every so often a flapping black wing or craning neck could be seen in the rise of a wave, but Parnell kept a firm grip and swam on. Out beyond the marker buoy he released the swan, pointed it towards Madagascar and, to the cheers of his beach fans, began swimming back to shore. He caught a wave and rode it in. Somersaulting out of it, he cleared his nose, adjusted his trunks and modestly acknowledged the applause of the beach urchins and his new friends. They were smiling a little too broadly, however. On the beach, flicking the unfamiliar sea water from its tail feathers, sat the swan.

Parnell looked surprised, then determined. He stamped the water from a blocked ear, lurched up to the swan, grabbed it up and set off again towards the sea. On the way it hissed aggressively and pecked his ear. He was clasping it tightly to his side but one wing flapped free and beat furiously, tousling his hair. Sandy kids danced around him, shrieking, and the Labrador began leaping up and barking. To this noisy circus the visitors offered smart suggestions. Geraldine looked embarrassed for her father but she was also half-smiling at the cracks and hubbub.

By now most people on the beach were watching the drama of the reluctant swan and pointing to Parnell slowly side-stroking out through the breakers. All the way the bird's serpentine head could be seen striking at his face and neck. Three or four children ran up to his shelter, raided it for free surf shooters and paddled them out after him.

In the deep Parnell again released the bird. This time he gave it a shove and watched it begin paddling away from land. He trod water for a while to make sure it kept swimming. Then he slowly began his long swim back to shore. He struck out for a big breaker, but it broke over him and he had to swim hard against its back-wash. On the beach people were clapping and cheering ironically. The visitors led the applause. 'The Swan King!' one of them shouted. In the middle of the crowd, which was making way for it with squeals and laughter, the swan waddled, hissing and snapping viciously.

Parnell plodded ashore with hair in his eyes and mucus trailing from a nostril. An ear was bleeding. He didn't swear or say a word. He picked his way through the people, wiping his nose. He got back to the shelter before Geraldine, turned to her and the lifesavers and fixed his eyes on her. 'Get back in here,' he ordered.

According to the police evidence in the newspapers Parnell arrived at the surf club very late that night, after the dance to

21

celebrate the surf championships, with a jerrycan of petrol. The club lost two surfboats and most of its reels and equipment in the fire. Drunkenness was taken into account, and his past record of fine community service — as the judge put it. The arson conviction got him four years.

All this was scandal enough for that time and place, but three or four years passed and we were living in Sydney, where Dad had been transferred by his company, before Annie told me the story behind the story. Until Parnell was in prison Geraldine was loath to reveal it, and she swore Annie to secrecy. She told Annie her father had been sleeping with her for three years — since she was thirteen. She thought it wasn't so much the indignity of the swan affair which had set him off as her interest in the fair-headed lifesaver.

This grim revelation started Annie off on a new line of conjecture. 'It *was* lucky that Mummy didn't marry Kevin instead,' she said at first. Then she changed tack and got to wondering in a quirky, romantic frame of mind whether it mightn't indeed have been better for both of them. 'Maybe they would have made each other happy,' she said. 'She mightn't have died and he wouldn't have been unbalanced and frustrated.' She looked suddenly distant and I knew she was imagining Geraldine's three years. 'And, anyway, I would've been there,' she said.

Shark Logic

J ournal entry for 10 January (11.00 p.m.): Six months, four days now since my 'death'.

Today is John's tenth birthday, a day of reflection for me. I fought a strong urge to send him something, even just a card, but that's impossible in the circumstances. My telephone call last month (after the splurge in the bar) still worries me. When I heard Peter's voice my heart beat so fast I came to my senses and hung up without speaking.

'Hullo, hullo,' he said, 'Hullo?' a questioning rising inflection in his voice. His voice was cracking at the edges, on the verge of breaking. When I 'died' it was still a high-pitched child's voice. Just as well Marion didn't come to the phone, I may have spoken. I came very close to speaking to Peter. He sounded so near, not twelve hundred miles away, in a different State. The line was very clear. In one ear I heard Peter's voice, in the other the surf breaking not a hundred metres from the phonebox. I wondered if he could hear the surf. I went back to my flat very depressed.

I haven't recorded before that my flat is in an apartment block, 'The Pines', one block back from the beach. If there were pines here once they must have succumbed to the fatal sea breeze which is killing off the Norfolk Island pines on the ocean front. (The environmentalists say the sea spray is laden with detergent and oil particles and that, combined with the salt, this mixture poisons the trees. They just dry up and die from the bottom up.) The block was built in the days when these studio flats were called bedsitters or one-bedroom flats, a generation before they became bachelor flats. I suppose the flat hasn't changed in all that time — a bedroom-cum-living room and dining room is all it is. There's a tiny kitchen and a bathroom with a glimpse of the sea from the lavatory. From my main room window I have a view of Palm Street and part of the beer garden attached to the Hotel Pacific next door.

It's not fancy living, but I make do. For example, I can eat for nothing at the pie shop. The shop carries a big range: the usual mincemeat, then potato, steak-and-kidney, pork, curry, chicken, veal, onion, on the savoury side, and fruit mince, raspberry, loganberry, apple, black currant, lemon meringue, custard and so forth, on the sweet side. When I say 'pie shop' I should say 'specialty pie shop' because it's quite an operation. We sell hundreds a day. The day trippers on the ferries, the surfers and the pier fishermen are our best customers. My job is to unload the full pie trays from the bakery van each morning and stack them in the ovens, wash the trays, sweep and clean.

I provide the backroom 'muscle'. The backroom aspect of the job is important for me. The front-of-the-shop work is done by two girls, Tracey and Maria, and Mrs Moore, the manageress. We're on civil terms but we're not what you would call friendly. People on the coast are more cold and aloof than I expected. No one looks you in the eye. That suits my purposes perfectly. Tracey is a thin, freckled girl about sixteen or so; Maria is slightly older and Italian. Mrs Moore is tense, grey and fiftyish and apt to be a bad-tempered martinet on busy days. I do my job efficiently and energetically and don't let her get me down. I remember that I was known as a strict disciplinarian myself.

I should make it clear that from the day I 'died' I have not touched or even spoken warmly to any female.

✻ ✻ ✻

My life here after six months is as simple as I can make it. I get up at eight, shower and eat some fruit. I do fifteen minutes transcendental meditation. Since I grew the beard I don't waste time shaving. My flat is only two blocks from the shop so I'm at work reading the morning paper in the loading bay when the bakery truck pulls up at nine. Because we all work through the lunch hour — our busiest period — we finish at four, sometimes earlier. Mrs Moore stays till after five doing the book work. Sometimes of a humid afternoon I sympathise with her. I know the pinch of responsibility, the hundred-and-one niggling pressures of authority. She must envy us our early departures — Maria and Tracey whipping off their green uniforms and sailing gaily out the door to meet their strangely dressed boyfriends, me putting on my sunglasses and fisherman's cap and wandering down the esplanade to the beach.

It has become part of my routine to walk along the beach after work, from the southern to the northern end and back, a distance of about three miles. During my walk I think things over as calmly as I can, using my breath exhalation relaxation techniques.

I've revised my plans; I can't live here. I think I will buy an air ticket to New Zealand. There are no immigration problems with New Zealand. 'Joe Forster' would have no passport or visa worries. Here, I'm still uneasy with the name. I keep reminding myself I need to be more cunning in my planning. I have to be constantly watchful for familiar faces in the crowds of summer tourists. I have to stay out of bars. I don't trust myself when I've had a few scotches; I could confide in some garrulous barfly. There is always the possibility of being spotted by someone from home. Even more likely is that I could become maudlin and lonely and initiate the contact myself.

After my walk along the beach I return to the flat via the fish shop where I buy some snapper or jewfish for dinner. I eat my meals at my window overlooking Palm Street. There is plenty to see out there, on some nights there is more activity than on the television. The coast is not what I had expected. Not only is the pace faster, but there is a careless, violent hedonism here that astonished me at first.

Last night two girls in bikinis were fighting in the street. They careered out of the Sun'n'Surf beer garden next door screeching drunk and began clawing at each other just under my window. Apparently they were both keen on the same youth, a big blond oaf who stood by with his laughing friends, egging them on until the police broke it up. On hot nights the streets don't clear until well after midnight. Even small half-dressed children are still shrieking up and down the pavements while their parents get drunk in the beer garden.

When I can't face the beach night-life, the coarse aimless lives, I close my window, pull the blind, turn on my electric fan and meditate. Behind and inside my contemplation the electric bass from the rock group in the beer garden throbs like an amplified pulse.

A life spent largely inland has made me awed and fascinated by the sea. The minutiae of a rock pool — the anemones, crabs and imperceptibly creeping limpets — can absorb me even in my worst depressions. I crouch like a child poking anemones with sticks, trickling sand into their cringing tendrils. The sea mystifies me. What caused thousands of sea-urchins, for example, to suddenly turn up the other morning clogging every tidal pool? When there had been no storm, when no other marine creature seemed affected by the mysterious disturbance which had agitated the sea-urchins. Even enterprising Omar, my landlord, whose Middle Eastern pragmatism has reasons for everything, had no answer to the sea-urchin mystery, though this didn't stop him and his cronies from scooping up as many of the creatures as they could stuff into buckets and sugarbags.

'What are you going to do with those?' I asked Omar. The things are rumoured to be poisonous; even a graze from their spikes festers instantly. Omar was thigh-deep in a sea pool wearing pink dish-washing gloves. Picking up spiky balls with a steady, sweeping motion, he looked up at me patiently. 'Eat!' he said aggressively. 'A bottle of beer and these, bloody good, Joe.' His gloves reminded me of a housewife in a detergent commercial. Cracking a sea-urchin on a rock while its spines retracted in surprise, he threw back his head and drained the creature like an egg.

Intrigued as I am by the ocean, I am not an enthusiastic surf swimmer. Living most of my life in the Tablelands, I prefer lake or river swimming. I'm a still-water man. Surf and tides turn malign too suddenly, waves dump you, sandbanks crumble in the current, undertows can catch you unawares. The local council maintains a swimming pool at the north end of the beach and I generally swim there. I have ventured into the ocean of course, usually on scorching days when the pool is jammed with children. It isn't the waves or undertow that worry me when I do, however — it's sharks.

I imagine they're everywhere. In every kelp patch, in the lip of every breaker, I sense a shark. Every shadow and submerged rock becomes one; the thin plume of spray in the edge of my vision is scant warning of its final lunge.

Of course my anxiety is not supported by statistics. There has not been a fatal shark attack on a swimmer in this strip of ocean since 1936. We have the best figures of any stretch of coastline. I keep newspaper cuttings on the subject. I have one clipping, *Meshing Cuts Shark Risk to Minimum,* in which a marine biologist asserts that the risk of being killed by a shark is the same as dying from a bee sting.

The reason for the low risk factor these days is meshing.

Meshing contractors regularly set nets off the beach to catch sharks, thus reducing the numbers in the area and the risk of attack. The nets don't close off sharks' access to the beach; the idea is to prevent them from establishing a habitat. The shark is denied territory.

It is hard to argue against the efficiency of this system when the annual fatality rate since its inception is zero. I actually see the meshing contractor out there in his boat as I'm walking after work, winding in his nets, motoring to a different site, re-setting them. But the nets are not set right across the beach. The beach is not closed off to sharks. I am a logical man and I have no trouble imagining a shark sensing me splashing about in the shallows and swimming in from the deep via a route where there is no net and, admittedly against large odds, biting me in halves.

There is an aquarium here with sharks on display. As the day trippers round the Point on the ferry the first landmark they see is the fifteen-foot black tin shark on the roof of Sealand and the sign announcing 'Savage Live Sharks'. Sealand doesn't bother advertising its turtles and stingrays, knowing it's the sharks that bring in the customers. I must admit to paying my admission to Sealand with the same morbid enthusiasm I felt thirty years ago entering the Police Department's tent at the local Agricultural Show to ogle severed hands, death masks of notorious nineteenth-century criminals and infamous murder weapons.

There were hints of seepage in the grey cement walls. The aquarium's windows streamed with condensation. Through misty glass children strained to peer beyond the scarred tuna and mundane yellowtail passing by, seeking the scary stuff. Then a shark appeared, grey, sleek, straight out of a TV documentary, a horror movie, and drifted past my face so slowly I saw its scars and the tiny parasites on its belly, even the opening and closing of its gills stirring the faint weed shreds on its skin.

The children oohed and aahed and jerked back from the windows. The shark cruised on, and five or six other sharks of all sizes gradually materialised from the murk and drifted after it.

You notice the teeth first, then the eyes. Sharks keep their mouths slightly open all the time, their lips drawn back from those irregular, sharply serrated teeth. The eyes, cold as a machine's, are also kept open. They are not savage eyes exactly — there is no jungle glint — they are just cold. I don't wish to be anthropomorphic, but I think they are the cruellest eyes in Nature.

I am drawn back to the aquarium regularly. I view the sharks through the windows and then I climb to the roof of the aquarium, in the sunshine, and look down on its open surface where the turtles rise, snorting. Looking down into the tank all you see are the ripples and whorls of the turbulence below. The sharks' fins never break the surface as they do in cartoons; there are no sinister black triangles cutting through the water. The water's greenish transparency turns black up there. All the creatures are invisible. Then a stingray's nonchalant wing tip breaks the surface, a turtle's mossy flipper, and the tension is relieved for a second before the surface settles again. On the roof everything is concentrated for me, my decision, my direction of my fate, my chosen loneliness. Up there only a low railing separates me from the water. Always I have the same infantile portentous sensation as I look down into the tank. There is the thrill of knowing they are endlessly circling down there and that there is the potential for me to jump in.

After six months there is nothing more in the newspapers, not that my disappearance made more than seven or eight paragraphs in the interstate editions. Those stories mentioned only that Mrs Cole-Adams had been the last person to see me, that I had dictated a short memo to her for the Bursar, remarked that I wanted to do a spot of trout fishing at Bourneville before dark, and left the school at 4.30. It was customary for me to go fishing once or twice a week, the papers correctly reported. The Rover was found parked by the spillway, one wader turned up three miles down-river near Tom's Dog Bridge — that was all. I certainly threw the rod away as well, presumably some local reprobate is now fishing with it.

I am still furious that one of the Sunday rags suggested that the school's financial affairs were reportedly kept 'in a casual manner'. I had to rein in a peculiar impulse to harangue the editor there and then. The papers referred to the unsuccessful search by the police and the Bourneville Volunteer Bushfire Brigade and the dragging of the Candlestick River. A month or so later a small item noted that the Board of Governors was advertising for a new headmaster.

Recording this tonight makes my heart race and a throbbing, claustrophobic feeling almost overcomes me. It has nothing to do with today's emotional and physical strains — I'm at loggerheads with myself. I have shrugged off my old life and its pressures, but too much of the provincial headmaster still clings to me. I am stupidly jealous of my replacement. I don't feel as I had expected, not as 'Joseph Forster' should feel. Perhaps the name was too romantic a choice for me. I am too conservative and this is not a romantic place. But it was the only name that occurred to me, considering the role of Conrad and Forster in my life over the years. After twenty years teaching Conrad it's ironic that I should be the one influenced by him. It's not likely that too many of my graziers' and country bank managers' stolid sons have followed the example of the Giant in Exile.

I still think New Zealand would suit me better. I understand it's about ten years behind the times. I'm not mocking myself — I feel somehow out of my era on the coast. I expected sun and serenity here. The grubby amorality, the lack of manners, saddens me. If I crystallised my impressions I would say that all the Englishness has gone. New Zealand is still very English, more so than England from what you hear these days. I suppose it is silly, but in my idealised daydreams New Zealanders all wear natural fibres, speak without stridor, play manly sports, entertain in their homes, eat roast lamb and mint sauce, go to bed early and read English literature.

Sometimes I find discarded hypodermic needles in the sand, some of them bloody, on Sunday mornings.

I was thinking about New Zealand when I left the shop this afternoon and set off for my usual walk along the beach. There was still a sting in the sun and the sand was hot when I removed my shoes. Smells from the seafront fried food shops hung in the air. The beach had an abused appearance: the sand was everywhere scuffed from the day's holiday crowds and littered with their refuse. The dying pines and the weather-beaten stucco-cement apartment blocks facing the ocean were starting to throw shadows across the beach. On the shore the afternoon tide was turning, levelling the children's deserted sand castles into muddy corrugations. Sodden bits of plastic, ice-cream wrappers and drink cans bobbed in the shallows. In front of me two fishermen were worming. One dragged a lump of decayed meat on a string back and forth over the wet sand and, every so often when a worm's head popped up, his companion bent quickly down, grabbed it with a hook affair, pulled the worm out and dropped it into a tin. The worms here are huge — twelve, eighteen inches long. As a fisherman myself I suppose I should have been in accord with this bait gathering, but today it revolted me.

The ocean, flat and soupy, felt tepid around my ankles. This is the time of day, the season, the temperature, I thought, peering out to sea, when most shark attacks occur — just before dusk when the fish schools come inshore to feed. Heedlessly, clumps of wilted-looking people were still arriving at the beach and throwing themselves into the water. I stood watching the sea, imagining the shark out there alerted by the splashing and the greasy slick of hundreds of bodies. I foresaw the subsequent panic with great clarity: the immense jolt and subsequent tearing and wrenching of flesh. Though no more than three or four inches deep in the sea, I stepped out onto dry sand.

As I walked further north away from the official bathing area the beach became less crowded, the swimmers spaced wider apart. A party of five or six foreigners was boisterously kicking a soccer ball about, making loud cries and generally showing off. Their podgy women sat on a blanket in their tight swimsuits giggling and regarding them admiringly. One man began walking on his hands and the women clapped and whistled. The other men, amiably jealous, pelted him with sand and the soccer ball until he fell over, thrashing wildly. Their rowdiness and flying sand annoyed me. Running skittishly from the others, his hair full of sand, one of them tumbled into me, thudding heavily into my side.

'Do you mind?' I said.

By now my mood was very low. I would have given up the walk and returned to my flat, but I knew how hot and stuffy it would be. And the idea of the emptiness and loneliness there today weighed on me. The image of myself at the window peering down on the vulgarities of the street was grotesque. I put some distance between the foreigners and myself, sat on a clean patch of sand and tried to think optimistically of my revised plans. My usual vision of New Zealand, of tweedy, peaceful people, beautiful scenery and grazing sheep, seemed an absurdity, like something from a 1950s travelogue.

No sooner had I sat down than two teenage couples sauntered up and flopped down nearby. Though no older than fourteen or fifteen they instantly embraced with great ardour and were soon writhing in the sand, each couple's loins locked together. I looked away, tense and embarrassed. Out to sea, just inside the line of breakers, a man was waving cheerily. Bobbing in the broken water, he was waving in my direction and calling out, 'Hoy, hoy.'

I glanced at the petting teenagers. 'Is that man calling you?' They looked up briefly, muttered something and fell back on each other. Squinting back over his shoulder, one boy said, 'He's waving to you.' He cackled coarsely. They all giggled. One of the girls said, 'Cop his funny cap.' The man did wave at me again. 'Hoy, hoy,' he cried softly. Dark hair hung in his eyes. Only his head and one waving arm were visible.

'He's in trouble,' I said. The boys and girls looked up again, but stayed petulantly in each other's arms. The man in the sea was waving less vigorously. 'Hoy,' he said once more as he began to sink.

I took off my shirt, cap and sunglasses and ran into the ocean in my trousers. The water was surprisingly cold. Small floating shreds of plastic and paper touched my arms and sides. I was conscious of these sensations, of my pants flapping uncomfortably, of my spine turning cold with fear, as I swam to the man, grabbed him around the chin and slowly side-stroked back to shore. Middle-aged and stocky, he was a sagging load and by the time I could stand I was panting with exhaustion.

'OK?' I asked, steadying him as we walked through the shallows. He brushed the hair from his eyes and burst into tears. I supported him until we stepped from the water. He patted my arm in thanks and, shaking his head, stumbled up the beach towards the group with the soccer ball. As I gathered my belongings and left the beach the teenagers clapped ironically.

When I got back to the flat I changed my clothes, went to the pub and drank several double scotches. By closing time I had come to the decision to ring home. At home it would be only eight o'clock. I willed John, the birthday boy, to answer the phone, but I told myself I was prepared for whatever happened. I don't know quite what I planned — just to listen and send loving thoughts back along the wire. Perhaps more. Marion would be washing the dishes no more than six or eight feet from the telephone. I was deathly exhausted with it all. I wanted to give up, to speak, to return.

I walked urgently to the public phonebox, past Sealand, on the beach front. The aquarium was dark and silent. The night surf boomed as usual, furtive shadows flitted on the beach. I heard the panting of running figures, grunts, cackling laughter. The phone rang for ten or fifteen seconds before it was answered. My heart beat so heavily I could hardly breathe.

'Yes?' a voice said, abruptly and assertively. 'Hullo! The Cameron residence! Hullo!' Peter's adolescent breaking voice had a crass defiant edge to it, an independence I didn't recognise. As he thumped down the telephone receiver I could sense the exasperated obscenity on his lips.

Baby Oil

Anthea had been living with Brian in Paddington for almost three years when she began an affair with Max in June. Anthea and Max met on a fashion shoot in Noumea. He was not the usual photographer her magazine used for fashion assignments, but Gunter was in Mauritius for *Vogue* and Max stood in. By the time they boarded their U.T.A. jet for Sydney a week later they were talking, rather surprisedly for such people as they recognised themselves, of being in love.

This affair was different from the other encounters Anthea had experienced while living with Brian. One afternoon at lunch soon after their return from New Caledonia, tanned and dreamy and still out of tune with the weather, she invited Max home, into her and Brian's house and, by extension, into her, their, bed.

In the past she had joined her lovers — a very catholic assortment with a rapid turnover — on afternoons at the Hilton or, on the rare occasion when one was single, at his place. In the spirit of frankness which marked the beginning of their affair she had told Max all this. The squalor of the bachelor flat had even added a *frisson* then, Max guessed, but only before the act — and there would never have been a return visit.

Anthea admitted to Max that her willingness to make love to him in her own bed was an indication of her strength of feeling for him, their spiritual and physical closeness. Their star signs were also terrifically compatible.

'We're kindred souls,' she said, kneading his buttocks in the lift going down from the New Hellas after lunch. She had also mentioned (rather defensively, he thought), 'I believe my body is mine to do with as I like.' Brian, a daily political cartoonist whom Max had never met, worked long hours on several publishing projects, and she travelled constantly, so the opportunities to uphold her belief were numerous.

Max could understand why someone wanted their lovers away from the domestic hearth. But having decided to break her usual rule she showed amazing *sang froid*, he thought, in drawing him urgently by the hand into the bedroom and onto the bed beneath a framed skiing holiday photograph of her with Brian, both beaming in red sweaters, cosy and radiant in the snow.

She was even more ardent than in Noumea. Her practice showed, her lean, whippy skills by no means subdued by the presence of Brian's accoutrements around them: pens, opened mail, coins and keys on the bedside table, Brian's *New Statesmans*, *Guardian Weeklys* and *New York Review of Books* stacked beside it, even a pair of Brian's red underpants hanging on his wardrobe doorknob. If she suffered any pangs of conscience at these souvenirs, at the juxtaposition of Brian's happy picture and Max's naked body, it didn't show.

It occurred to Max that as Anthea had obviously planned for them to return here after lunch this particular afternoon, but had not removed the more intimate traces of Brian's occupation, even the rather blatant note of the discarded underpants, that maybe she got a kick out of it. Or perhaps she was just a sloppy housekeeper. Anyway, the combination of this selective insensitivity and her carnality held enough intrigue for him. And Brian's bits and pieces didn't unduly concern him; perhaps, if he were honest, they even added a spark.

He was right, there was a perceptible change in her love-making now; not in her techniques exactly, but she was slightly less romantically swept away, even more lustful than under the Pacific palms. The face was not expressive with tropical wonder. She had changed up a gear. Her in-bed personality now was one of impassive sexual hunger. She burbled sweet obscenities, her body was warm and responsive, but there was something almost neutral in the eyes.

'Just wonderful, my darling,' she said afterward, fetching them tumblers of Chablis. Max sipped, and flipped through a *New Statesman*. Very dull lay-out, no photographs to speak of, a couple of anti-Thatcher cartoons. Brian was presently in Alice Springs or somewhere doing a book of drawings of Aborigines. Presumably she washed the sheets before his return. Maybe while she was at it she could throw in the bloody underpants.

A little later, for the encore, she reached up to the bedstead for a bottle of baby oil. Slowly anointing them, she whistled softly at his pleasure. She had obviously made a speciality of this. Under a film of oil her tan glistened. On her brown breasts the nipples were big silver coins, then their slippery cones darted everywhere — even the backs of his knees, the soles of his feet didn't escape their touch — until he couldn't differentiate between tongue and nipple. Anthea glided knowingly over him, they slid together, undulating like an ocean swell, rolling and curving towards shore. Owing to the wild buffeting of the bed Brian's coins and keys rattled and danced.

As their affair intensified over the next weeks Max spent a lot of time in Anthea's bedroom. Emboldened by the intensity and intimacy of lunch they would kiss on restaurant stairs, hail taxis with incautious exuberance, and she would draw him home to Paddington. He succumbed gladly to the force. What could match the thrill of the cab ride along Oxford Street, thighs pressed conspiratorially together; the anticipation as she fished in her handbag for the key? Max's senses sang, his hormones fizzed. The teasing abandonment of the kiss inside the door! Her fellatio attacks on him in the hallway! (The sensual relaxation of her lower lip almost floored him.) His heightened perception amazed him. Her textures, smell and taste were uniformly exquisite.

It went even further than Anthea. Max's general attention to detail was never more acute than in the opening minutes of their afternoons together. Even as he entered the bedroom and began undressing every corner of the room instantly registered on him. He noted the current disarray of male and female clothing or any minor adjustments to the furnishings since his last visit — the addition of a TV set in front of the bed, for example — which hinted at domestic conviviality. Conviviality was the alleged keynote of the Anthea-Brian relationship. Implied was plain old friendship rather than romantic sexuality. That was all right; Max could live with conviviality.

'He makes me laugh,' she'd volunteered to Max. 'That's all.' He knew better than to pursue the matter. He was never quite sure what women meant when they said that. It sounded platonic but he suspected it covered the whole range to one hundred per cent sexual. Women were so wonderfully dishonest and dismissive when it suited them. In the face of this treachery Max quite often felt more in league with the husband or boyfriend he was cuck-olding than with the woman in question — equally, eternally ignorant of the extent of female fraudulence.

Objects still registered on his consciousness as he climbed into bed — even the bed coverings themselves — and created their own spun-off meanderings. The erotic suggestion he'd got one afternoon from black satin sheets, for instance, was partly allayed by the realisation that they were *their* satin sheets and that at one time at least they had thought black satin sheets would be a sexy thing to experience.

'Kinky,' he joked, the day of the sheets.

'A bit of a cliché, aren't they?' said squirming, sliding Anthea, slippery enough as she was.

The oil plus the sheets made purchase difficult. The sheets did not return.

'I love you,' she told Max often, whenever he looked serious.

'I love *you*,' he repeated.

The State Department gave Brian a trip to the United States for being a pace-setter in his branch of the media — and to keep him on-side. Max rejoiced. His afternoons with Anthea quickly formed a pattern. They managed to meet about three days a week throughout August. They would rush to bed and make love. Then Anthea, pulling on one of Brian's T-shirts, would totter downstairs and bring them up glasses of wine. Once, returning to bed, she stretched to remove the shirt and Max saw for an instant the light catch the shine of his moisture on the inside of her thigh. The image of this peaceful interval remained fixed photographically in Max's mind when they were apart: their quiet bodies settled obliquely across the bed as they murmured and sipped wine and laughed softly. He ran a finger along her vulnerable hip. A cool breeze played with the net curtains. The cat rearranged itself in the laundry basket.

Before long she would take his glass from him, reach for the baby oil and slyly, languorously, begin Stage Two.

Cool rain. Drops as distinct as purity fell on his thirsty skin. Sighing, Max reclined as she dripped oil on his penis, spread oil on her nipples with a studious familiarity and then caressed herself with him. Her New Caledonian tan had faded; she was the shade of peaches. The silken delicacy of her touch approached no touch at all. Though her lubricity made it redundant, Anthea passed him the oil to caress her thighs. He dropped some oil into his hand — one droplet — and his heart jumped. The bottle was empty.

Two days before it had been a quarter full. Squeezing hard, Max forced out the last drop of oil. He let it fall in her navel.

Perceptibly, even against Max's inclination, Brian's possessions and knick-knacks began to get on his nerves. It became an effort to use the bathroom, to shower after their love-making, with Brian's *New Yorkers* stacked by the lavatory, his *Eau Sauvage* on the shelf, the ubiquitous red underpants hooked over the doorknob. In bed he would look up from her face or breasts or thighs into the tanned faces of the amiable skiing duo. Her hair was longer then, darker, her face rounder. He hated the Anthea in the photograph. He made love with great passion and they both cried out with equal vehemence. Afterward she gave him a quizzical look but said only, 'I love you.'

One late August afternoon when Anthea left the bed for the bathroom, Max, compelled, took Brian's pen from the bedside table and marked the oil level in the current bottle. Its label said:

Johnson's
Baby
Oil
PURE – MILD – GENTLE
Johnson & Johnson
200 ml

Max made a small spot of ink alongside the J for Johnson's at the top of the label. Replacing the bottle, his pulse racing, he saw the oil as suddenly volatile, with a sheen like gin.

It came as no surprise to him, though set his heart beating in his throat with a delicious, frightening anguish as if to choke him, to note two days later that the oil level was well below his mark. It was actually between the B of Baby and the O of Oil. Following their afternoon in bed, a feverish, almost savage exercise that left them both drenched and shaky, Max again marked the oil level, now just above the P for PURE.

Three tense days passed before they could next go to bed together. Max had hardly slept. Each dawn, jogging red-eyed and heavy-limbed along Bondi beach, he decided resolutely to end the affair. Each morning she rang his studio cheerily to say, 'I love you.' He resisted saying it.

'Tell me you love me,' she wailed.

He had trouble visualising her at her shiny green desk, a cigarette going between her bright nails, talking like this. 'I love you,' he said.

'Good.'

On the third day when Max entered the bedroom the bottle may as well have been the only object in the room. They could have been fucking on bear skins or broken glass. The label was turned to the wall but the oil level already seemed lower. The oil was as ominous as a sultry sea at dusk, tropically translucent before a storm. Its diffused whorls hid sharks, stingrays, venomous transparent mysteries. Max's senses almost exploded. As soon as Anthea went downstairs for the wine he snatched up the bottle. Of course the level was down, way below the P, almost to the next J.

When she returned he was subdued, flaccid as a jellyfish. 'When did Brian get back?' he asked, almost strangled by nonchalance.

'He didn't.' Then she said, correcting herself, 'He comes and goes,' blushed and sniggered softly, a noise midway between embarrassment and coarseness, the most unattractive sound he had heard in his life.

She picked up quickly. 'Why do you ask?'

The essence was right out of him and he let it go. 'No reason.'

'I love you,' she said, staring into his eyes.

As the oil dripped on him he watched her face, impassive except for a small moué of sensuality. Fury revived his spirit and they collided in lust and high emotion. Coins and keys spun and jangled beside them. Later, while she went to the lavatory, he marked the bottle. The tiny dot, between the J and the 200 ml, took his final strength.

Max and Anthea had a passionate lunch at Doyle's, overlooking the slick spring Harbour. Behind clouds a pale sun hung over Watson's Bay. They held hands on the table, drank two bottles of Chardonnay, kissed in public, over-tipped and caught a taxi home to Paddington.

Max hadn't even undressed when he grabbed up the oil bottle right in front of her to examine it, stare at it. On the other side of the label, well below his last mark, almost at the bottom of the label, was a clearly inked cross which accurately recorded the present level in the bottle.

Looking for Malibu

'There is a growing tendency for Australians of a certain kind to seek the fulfilment of their lives or careers in America — and not just the well-publicised pop singers and tennis players. Whereas the creatively stifled and emotionally restless Australian middle classes of earlier generations "returned" to England or Europe for cultural sustenance, the new film-makers, artists, academics and business entrepreneurs are increasingly forming expatriate communities in California and New York.

'Yesterday the Australian Consul-General held a party at his Jackson Street residence to celebrate the local release of Breaker Morant, the latest movie from Down Under, and no less than eighteen Aussie film-makers, actors, writers and painters were counted imbibing the excellent Australian wines . . .'

San Francisco Chronicle

After the consulate party David Lang took Richard Bartho, the Sydney film-maker, and Peter Boyle, the Sydney department store family's black sheep, both visiting from Los Angeles, for a drink at the Vesuvio bar.

The Langs had been living in San Francisco for twelve months and had their favourite haunts. David, an architect, had just completed a sabbatical year at Stanford and Berkeley, with a side visit to Harvard and a cold, drizzly fortnight at the University of Oregon at Eugene, and he and his family were shortly to return to Australia. Back home, where he lectured at Sydney University and had his own practice, and his wife Angela taught screen-writing at the Film and Television School, they had known Bartho for many years.

David hadn't met Boyle before. He knew of him only through the financial press and the Sunday social columns — and random dinner party conversations where the doings of the buccaneer rich were either extolled or savaged. He certainly hadn't mixed in his circle of right-wing establishment playboys. Two or three years before he'd heard of him suddenly resigning his chairmanship, selling all his shares in the Boyle Emporium Limited back to his family for four or five million dollars and moving to Southern California. Bartho and Boyle had also never previously met.

But a foreign country — even America — makes for convivial compatriots. At the Vesuvio, Bartho and David had several palate-cleansing beers, Boyle had a couple of scotches and the three men joked and hedged around onto common ground. This was the usual expatriate discussion on green cards, permanent residential status. Boyle had a green card, the others four-year visas. Bartho then brought up the subject of film investment as a tax incentive.

'Stop buttering him up,' David said to him. Boyle laughed.

'I can't afford to lose an opportunity,' Bartho complained. 'How long do you think this gravy train's going to last?'

Before long it was dark and David suggested dinner. The others agreed enthusiastically and they strode in high spirits down Columbus Avenue to the Washington Square Bar and Grill.

'You'll like it,' David told Bartho. 'Coppola eats there.'

'Jeezus! He's on the skids.'

As soon as they sat down Bartho ordered vintage Dom Perignon. 'All part of the image,' he announced. Then he addressed Boyle. 'I've been trying to think who you remind me of. I've decided it's the young Sydney Greenstreet.'

'That's an improvement,' Boyle said, lighting a cigar. 'I used to look like the young King Farouk.'

Bartho laughed loudly and several diners turned around. 'Actually, you still do,' he said. 'And the young Sydney Green-street. Perhaps it's the white suit.'

'How are you doing in Hollywood with your diplomatic ways?' Boyle asked.

'Great. The moguls are suckers for the brash young Aussie bit. Don't think I don't load on the accent, either. I come on ultra-straight, butch and scruffy and they just fall over. No Balmain irony in Hollywood, cobber.'

'Don't underestimate the moguls,' Boyle said. 'Moguls can be trouble, son.'

'That's just what I was telling Sherry Lansing at Fox yesterday.'

Boyle leaned over the table to David. 'This boy is an original,' he said.

'You better believe it!' Bartho hooted.

'You may go far.'

'Only as far as my American Express card,' Bartho said, ordering more champagne.

David couldn't tell them how refreshing he found this abrasive boozy banter after the hot-tubbing, laid-back silkiness of Californian academe. It made him nostalgic for Australia and its laconic clubbiness. Maybe he wasn't the expatriate type. They ate, joked, drank Bartho's champagne, walked back up Columbus for cognacs and coffee at the Tosca, exchanged phone numbers and disappeared into the night in different taxis.

Next morning David had an evil hangover. Angela was sympathetic, perhaps because of its nationalistic origins. He considered, gratefully, that a couple of years ago she wouldn't have been. They had been together fifteen years. Two years before, under the swamp-gum in their Mosman garden, away from the children's ears, they had talked of separating, but the discussion itself, conducted around mugs of coffee in those green and secure surroundings, had scared them out of it. Angela's private definition of fear, enunciated that Sunday morning under the gum tree, was finding a letter from another woman in his coat pocket. His was discovering her in an intimate restaurant bar in earnest conversation with a strange man. The year in America had been organised by him and perceived by them both as a chance for reconcilement and new harmony.

To a degree it had worked. San Francisco had been a qualified success. Angela loved the city, so much that sometimes it seemed it had insinuated itself between them. He liked the Bay Area well enough and had enjoyed prowling around Berkeley, but he was looking forward to going home; she could have stayed forever. It was their children, Paul, Helena and Tim, especially Paul, the eldest, who hadn't taken to the place.

It was Paul who suffered most from the vagaries of its much

51

vaunted 'lifestyle'. He endured the bussing to a distant high school in the Mission district, where he was regarded by the school's Latino and black drug and weaponry entrepreneurs as an egregiously unhip Anglo novelty. And it also depressed him closer to home, where there were few teenagers in the landscape. Their apartment block on Sacramento and Laguna had an elaborate security system to protect its snooty elderly tenants specifically from the likes of him: they eyed him like a mugger or a mainliner in the lobby. Early on, when Paul crossed Sacramento Street to hit tennis balls in Lafayette Park, men with closely cropped hair kept idling by into the bushes, whistling and making flattering remarks. Red-faced with anger and embarrassment, he'd burst back into the apartment and refused to return, even to play tennis with his father. He drooped around the living room reading surfing magazines and crunching peanut brittle, muttering cynically about the trysting males and Pacific Heights dowagers walking their Shih Tzus and Lhasa Apsos below the window. He daily gave the impression California had let him down.

His father agreed that San Francisco gave kids short shrift. 'Southern California's different,' he sympathised. 'The Beach Boys, Hollywood, surfing. We're going to do all that stuff before we leave. But this is really interesting here. Three blocks down is Fillmore Street. You've heard of Bill Graham's Fillmore Auditorium where Janis Joplin and Big Brother and the Holding Company used to record? All those great San Francisco rock traditions? They were just down the street.'

'I don't know them,' Paul said.

'You've heard of the Vietnam war, I suppose? The peace and love movement started in Golden Gate Park. That's where the whole protest movement got going with Joan Baez, Bob Dylan and Co.'

'Protesting against what?'

David Lang stared for a while out the window. On the steep

incline of Laguna Street a plump young man dressed in a solar topee and tight gold shorts and carrying a three-foot long blaring tape player, sped down on roller skates. 'Anyway, Southern California's different,' he said.

One of the minor ambitions of his life was to swim at Malibu.

David was mildly surprised to receive a phone call from Peter Boyle two days later. He had been delayed on business in San Francisco, he said, suggesting lunch. David's sabbatical commitments were over and they were planning their Southern California holiday for the following week. The scheme was to drive down Highway 1 to Los Angeles and on to San Diego, taking it easy, no more than a hundred miles a day, with stopovers at Monterey, Big Sur, San Simeon, San Luis Obispo and Santa Barbara. He wanted to motor through the redwood canyons of the Pacific Coast Highway with the mountains plunging into the windswept ocean at his shoulder, just like in the *Sunset Guide*. But that was a week off, he could manage lunch, and they decided to meet at the Vesuvio. 'They'd never believe this in Sydney, you and Peter Boyle so chummy,' Angela said.

When he arrived Boyle was sitting at the bar drinking an Anchor Steam beer. There was no white suit today. He was dressed in Levis and a khaki bush jacket and his hair looked longer and floppier. He blended into the raffish atmosphere of the bar. David felt over-dressed in his tweed jacket. It was his bar and he was the one out of kilter.

'Dave, how're you doing?' Boyle greeted him. David noted the Americanism 'doing', rather than the usual Australian 'going'. Boyle seemed altogether more Californian today, very San Francisco, even to the stack of paperbacks at his elbow. 'I just dropped in to the City Lights next door,' he said. 'L.A.'s not so big on bookstores, much less Ferlinghetti.'

David realised he didn't know Boyle at all. Nevertheless his first impression of him did not include avant-garde poetry, or jeans and bush jackets for that matter. He was vaguely curious why Boyle should pursue their relationship, but guessed at loneliness or even homesickness. Boyle probably sought him out mainly on the basis of nationality. Not that it mattered. They chatted amiably and then walked up the street to lunch.

During an Italian meal and a glass of Chianti, however, David felt it reasonable to ask him why he had moved to California. Immediately he felt he had overstepped some mark because Boyle stopped eating and sat with a forkful of veal poised in front of his face for a second before resuming, at the same time looking at David forcefully while he chewed.

He did reply though, with a distant smile. 'Pressure of one sort and another,' he said. 'I was under a bit of strain.'

'Any regrets?' David went on blithely. After all, it was Boyle who was directing this sociability. 'It must have been a difficult decision.'

Boyle shrugged. *Yes*, David thought.

'The company's going to the shit-heap now,' Boyle said. 'My brother's screwing it up, my uncle's screwing it up and my mother's retreated into her bloody bedroom and hasn't spoken to anyone since July. It's ripe for a takeover, sure as God made little apples. Myer will get it, Bond maybe, nothing surer.' His smile became even tighter. 'Hear that rumbling sound? That's my old man turning in his grave.'

Then he changed the subject so blatantly David could almost hear the gears clash. 'You mentioned you'd spent some time in Oregon recently. See any Australians up there or on the way? Northern California, Mendocino area perhaps?'

David said he hadn't. He felt this wasn't a random query, however.

'Just for your information, there's quite a few up there, living very quietly in their coastal hideaways.'

'Really? Dropouts, eh?'

'Very big dropouts. It's too hot for them in Australia.'

David liked gossip as much as anyone. 'Criminals?' he asked.

Boyle drained his glass. 'Not really, just your Eastern Suburbs *laissez faire* capitalists, old public schoolboys who like a snort and got in too deep.' He went on, 'It's rather funny.' A lank lock of black hair hanging in Boyle's eyes made him look surprisingly disarrayed. It hung down to his nose for what seemed an inordinate length of time before he wiped it back and poured more wine.

'Funny?'

'If their enemies were middle-class Australians they'd know where to look for them. You know something? When Australians run away they always run to the coast. They can't help it. An American vanishes, he could be living in New Mexico, Arizona, Colorado, the mountains, the desert, anywhere. Not an Australian — he goes up the coast or down the coast and thinks he's vanished without a trace.'

It was probably the wine, but David couldn't resist the joke. 'Where are you living in L.A., Peter?'

Boyle glinted a little. For a moment David thought he might be drunk. 'Malibu,' he said. 'On the beach at Malibu, home of the stars.'

To take the sting out of his query, David rapidly mentioned their forthcoming trip and that they were looking forward to surfing at Malibu. While he was rambling about their missing the beach and a proper summer and so forth, Boyle interrupted him gruffly.

'Be our guests,' he offered. 'We've got plenty of room. Fiona would love to meet you.' And while David was politely declining, pointing out the rowdiness of his children and the haphazardness of their plans, the other man put up a hand to silence him and declared, 'Actually, Fiona's coming up here tomorrow. You and your wife have dinner with us and we'll make the arrangements.'

If David had been a little surprised at Boyle's interest before, now he was taken aback. So was Angela. While they were dressing she asked, 'If we're being fêted by the Boyles up and down California, do I pretend Marin County-style or go as the All-Australian girl?'

'All-Australian girl, I think. They seem nostalgic for it.'

'Why are we doing this?' She was frowning as she threaded herself into her pantyhose.

'I don't know. Curiosity? Don't be antagonistic about it. He seems lonely, a bit cut adrift. What have we got to lose?' And also because back home Boyle was a big name and they were not long enough away not to be flattered at his attentions.

Their host had suggested a favourite restaurant in Chinatown. When the Langs arrived on the dot of 7.30 the others weren't yet there. When they arrived ten minutes later, Boyle's resemblance to the early Sydney Greenstreet was apparent to David too. It was the exotic backdrop, the ornate red and gold restaurant-Chinese archway framing them, which heightened the effect. Tonight Boyle was dressed in another creamy suit, a pink shirt and dark club tie, and his hair was slicked back in the thirties' manner. His wife was as tall as he. Fiona Boyle was lean and sharply pretty and appeared twelve or fifteen years younger than her husband. In one circumspect paragraph the social pages had recorded their marriage, his third and her second, about two years ago. Toward Angela and David her manner was instantly affable and attractive. She moved fluidly to their table, chatting in a broad Australian accent as if she had known them for years and was grateful to come across them.

Apologising for their lateness, Boyle announced, 'We ran into Jim Dunlop in the hotel lobby. He asked me if I could get him a girl. I hope you don't mind if they join us later?'

David and Angela looked at each other. 'Not at all,' they said together.

'A girl?' David laughed.

Boyle said, 'Silly old Jimmy. He's here with some Parliamentary delegation. He came up to me moaning plaintively, "I've got a list for New York and Washington but I don't have a number for San Francisco." He'd already struck out with the cocktail waitresses. Anyway, I got him someone.'

The meal passed slowly for David. The suspense of waiting for the arrival of the conservative Cabinet Minister and his 'date' was almost delicious. This was a stronger dose of nationalism than he'd expected. Meanwhile Angela and Fiona seemed to be hitting it off surprisingly well, given Angela's usual initial reserve. Boyle was also enjoying being host, becoming more expansive and assuming more authority by the minute. He had already taken it on himself — apparently when making the restaurant booking — to order Peking duck for everyone; now he was demanding a particular Napa Valley Chardonnay which the restaurant did not stock. 'Send out for it then, my man,' he dismissed the wine waiter. David squirmed at this sort of behaviour and also envied its perpetrator his clout and knowhow. A call-girl for a Cabinet Minister, an unavailable wine, it was all a cinch.

Discussing the events of the evening afterwards, David and Angela differed only on the colour of the call-girl's hair. He recalled her as a redhead; she insisted on brunette. They didn't disagree that she had been pleasant, modestly pretty, tastefully dressed and, as a former Berkeley political science student, possibly too intelligent a companion for the smirking political rake. She, Kathy, had got there first. The details of the minister's actual arrival were also agreed upon: they had both delighted in the nervous adjustment of the tie-knot in the doorway, the sudden little spring of feigned youth in the step, the look of confusion when confronted by three youngish, attractive women.

What fascinated David was the way Boyle had let him suffer. He had introduced them all only by first names. So Dunlop had squeezed between Fiona and Angela and trotted out all his dated suave ploys. He read the love lines in their palms, twinkled right and left, volunteered star signs and showered the table w .h innuendo. His hands were a blur of motion from knee to knee. Boyle leaned back in his chair and watched this performance with great satisfaction, letting fifteen or twenty minutes pass before he announced with great solemnity, 'Minister, may I present, at the far end of the table, Ms Molera, your companion for this evening.' David felt like clapping.

David and Angela also agreed that as neither of the Boyles had mentioned their staying with them at Malibu they would let the invitation, if one existed, lapse.

David was carrying luggage down to their second-hand Thunderbird when Helena called him up to the telephone. Fiona Boyle was calling from L.A. 'When can we expect you down here?' she asked.

He gathered his wits and rambled on once more about not inconveniencing them, and the loose nature of their schedule. 'Actually, we're leaving San Francisco in a minute.'

Fiona interrupted him. 'Look, we've got a big place on the beach and domestic help. It's no problem. Peter is counting on it,' she said. 'You'd be doing us both a favour.' She spoke lower into the phone. 'It would do him a lot of good, he's a bit down at the moment. He needs the distraction of a few friendly faces.'

What could he say? He thanked her and said to expect them a week from today.

'We look forward to seeing you,' she said brightly.

✳ ✳ ✳

The trip was not without its tensions. By the third day, at the edge of the Roman pool at the Hearst castle, Paul said loudly to his sister, 'Why don't you fall in and drown?' His accent carried across the terrace to at least two tourists other than his father, who gave him curious glances. Picking up the *frisson*, the tour guide announced that they could now smoke if they had to, but repeated her warning against touching the statues. She wore, David noticed, the same masculine green uniform as had their guide at Alcatraz. It accentuated her broad hips and gave her a rolling, Smokey-the-Bear gait up the wide staircases and along the patios.

'They're porous, you'll understand,' the guide said. 'No offence, folks, but each of us has this uric acid and ammonia in our skin and that Carrara marble just soaks it up like a sponge.'

David glared at his son. He watched him saunter morosely over to a drinking fountain and remove his maroon felt cap before bending over the faucet. The boy fancied himself in the cap; it had been his first American purchase, at Macy's, the day after their arrival. David had believed it an odd buy then, considering its irrelevance as a Californian fashion souvenir. This lack of novelty seemed not to have occurred to Paul. He'd barely had the cap off his head all year, and now, after wiping his mouth on his sleeve, he replaced it purposefully, pulling the peak low on his forehead. Today he had teamed the cap with a red 'Sex Wax' surfer's T-shirt, his only concession to the spirit of the holiday. He stood at the balustrade and, his chin jutting self-consciously, peered out over the pool and the San Simeon hills to the ocean.

A light Pacific haze lay across the sun and horizon. Ridiculously photogenic, two zebras, descendants of William Randolph's original herd, trotted suddenly over a knoll into camera range and stopped to graze. In the rush to the balustrade Helena came up to her father, remarking matter-of-factly, 'He hates me.' Squeezing her hand he turned back to the guide with a question on the zebras. In the corner of his eye was the silly defiant cap.

After the castle they had a picnic lunch on the beach at San Simeon. None of the other hundreds of castle tourists had considered this: chiefly Americans, they lined up for hot dogs and hamburgers and tacos at the concession stand in the parking area and stayed clear of the pebbly sand.

'They don't understand the beach culture,' David joshed with his elder son.

'Maybe they don't want to look like jerks hanging around where there's no surf,' Paul said. Despite everything, he had been very receptive to the American accent and slang. Grabbing a sandwich, he wandered down to the shore, head down, cap over his eyes.

'Can I come with you?' Helena called.

'With you?' echoed the baby, Tim.

'No!' Paul called back. The relentless word hung in the air. Helena's eyes sprang with tears.

'He really is too much,' Angela said. 'You'd better have a word with him, David.'

He said nothing. He had been avoiding scenes since they set off; he hated the way travelling scenes changed in shape and engulfed everything, like amoebas.

Angela's face was cool and affronted. With a sharp knife she dextrously peeled an apple and handed it to Helena. 'Go and collect some stones, darling,' she said. The unbroken peel momentarily retained the apple's sphericity. Angela was good at that trick. David thought briefly that she made the peel more important than the apple.

'Why should she want to collect stones?' he asked. He believed he was smiling mildly. 'Shells, yes.'

'The stones are pretty here. I read it in the *Sunset Guide*.'

'I don't want to collect stones,' Helena cried. 'I can't eat this

60

apple!' She dropped it in a trash can.

'Don't waste that good apple!' shouted her father. 'What a bloody waste!'

'You can all do as you like,' Angela said. 'Be as tiresome as you like.' She lay back on the rough sand and closed her eyes wearily. Timmy began to cry until his father picked him up. Low grey waves snapped against the pier.

Strangely, of all their stopovers before Los Angeles David could remember clearly only San Simeon and Santa Barbara when later recalling the trip's effect on their lives.

In Santa Barbara he was walking back from the motel sauna to their room. It was drizzling rain and Helena ran up to him flushed and with damp hair, exclaiming, 'Paul's going to play with me today! We're going to swim in the pool!' He could not tell her the weather was too bleak. He felt immeasurably sad, as sad as he had ever been.

Reloading luggage in the Thunderbird thirty minutes later he watched Paul and Helena playing out of the corner of his eye. His daughter, round and chubby in her swimsuit, bobbed in the shallow end of the pool, shrieking with happiness and gratitude. The boy was not actually *playing*, in the sense of sharing fun, he was just in the pool at the same time. Pale and stringy, he dived and swam with aggression and panache, as if making up for a lost indoor year. His angularity, his new American mumble, the long, flat feet slapping on the wet paving around the pool, were a stranger's. Light rain fell on the children's wet bodies. A smell of chlorine hung in the air. Around the terrace Mexican women pushed trolleys of bed linen, towels and detergent. Stacking their bags in the trunk, David noticed his hands were shaking.

Angela appeared by the car and said, 'Call the kids, will you?' He thought her make-up looked laboured this morning, a big effort for the final stretch and their arrival at the Boyles', he supposed.

He preferred the casual American look, the Northern Californian look. Wind-in-the-long-hair, little cosmetics. In the dim past she used to have this look herself. In her sleep her beauty, her serene, happy profile, had taken his breath away. When he called them, Helena whined and pleaded for more time but Paul climbed instantly from the pool without a word. His snappy obedience verged on insolence.

As they got into the car David said to his wife, 'You've got lipstick on your teeth.'

Even on the quieter coastal highway approaching Los Angeles they picked up energy from the traffic's increased momentum. At the sight of road signs from a hundred movies and cop shows everyone perked up and began chattering.

'You all asked for beaches, here're beaches,' announced David. 'This is where beaches were invented!' Paul began reciting them from the map: 'Leo Carillo State Beach, Zuma Beach, Malibu Lagoon, Las Tunas, Topanga, Will Rogers State Beach, Santa Monica, Venice, Manhattan, Hermosa, Redondo, Long Beach, Sunset, Bolsa Chica, Huntington, Newport, Corona Del Mar, Laguna . . . There're only two spots that interest me — Malibu and Huntington,' he said, but his eyes were shining.

Angela had her make-up purse out and was freshening the colour in her cheeks. She combed her hair, then suddenly squeezed his knee, an old warm gesture so currently unfamiliar that he almost jumped. 'Well, we made it,' she said. 'The old intrepid team.'

He squeezed hers back. Over her shoulder sea and sky fused in a dazzling milky light. On his side the highway bit into the muddy hills and periodically the car was diverted around landslides by barriers or road gangs. Angela read out the Boyles' address to him: 21 001 Pacific Coast Highway, Malibu. Dropping speed, he cruised past public beaches until the first beach houses appeared, perched together precariously on the cliffs and blocking the sea views.

David didn't know what he was expecting, a minor Hearst mansion perhaps, but he was unprepared for the weathered pine and stone structure clinging like a limpet to the hillside, its entrance flush to the highway and its sides closely abutting its neighbours. He stopped the car and announced himself in an intercom beside the high pine gate. After a delay during which he could hear someone breathing, he repeated his name. The gate swung open and he drove inside.

Once behind the gate they saw that outside appearances had been deceptive. The building on the street was just an annexe — perhaps servants' quarters — to a larger, contemporary pine and shingle house which squatted on latticed struts behind it facing the Pacific. Even though this building was at the most fifty yards from the highwater mark on its own beach, a swimming pool and a big redwood spa tub had also been set into the hillside, and bobbing in the pool, as the Lang family approached, was a naked man.

As they came tentatively nearer two things happened. The man giggled and climbed out of the pool, and a tiny dark woman came out of the house holding a growling German Shepherd by the collar. At the dog's appearance Tim began crying; Helena ran behind her father.

'What is this!' Angela cried.

'Mr and Mrs Boyle, please!' requested David. 'Mr Peter Boyle!'

The nude man, perhaps Mexican, switched on the hot tub, fumbled on the ground beside it for a joint, lit up and slowly settled himself in the oscillating foam. The woman with the dog also appeared to be Mexican. She wore a lemon housecoat and her sneakered feet and her grip on the collar looked insecure. Clasping one of the house struts to support herself, she cried, '*Vamos!*' and waved them away. The man shouted something at her, then

63

smiled happily at Angela. 'Babee,' he said, 'Honee,' and holding out his invitatory cigarette he groggily beckoned her to join him. His other hand was busy under the water.

'All go in the Mercedes!' the woman shouted. 'Nothing!' And needing her hands to gesticulate speedy departure, absence and nothingness, let go of the collar.

Angela screamed, the dog moved towards them very jerkily, literally in slow motion, for several steps, and then fell, frothing, on its side and died.

David found himself beside the dog and the woman. Some time in the recent past the dog had been shot in the head; the blood had crusted in its fur. The way the woman was weeping and holding its head in her lap put him in mind of the widow of a shot gunslinger. She had whisky on her breath and the smell of it brought him out of his detachment, the weird sensation that he was taking part in American television. 'They've gone, eh?' he asked unnecessarily. She nodded.

In the car no one spoke. David sat motionless behind the wheel for five minutes, then turned the car around and drove back to the Malibu public beach. 'This is Malibu,' he said. 'Go to it.'

Angela said she thought she could see a supermarket on the hill. 'I need a few things,' she said, and left, taking Tim with her.

'Are you surfing?' David asked Paul. The surf was middling and the sunlight behind the waves revealed a thin skein of kelp stretching intermittently along the shore. Two surfers were out on their boards; no one was swimming. In the distance a hang-glider drifted over the cliffs like a scrap of burnt paper. The boy shrugged. 'I'll have a look in the surf shop,' he said, and disappeared after his mother.

It was neither warm nor cool, sunny nor cloudy. The beach was unremarkable. In the bright milky light the pier stood out in sharp relief. David didn't swim. He and Helena walked out on the pier.

Her hand kept tightening its grip; she wouldn't let him go. Big grey eastern Pacific gulls wheeled silently over men cleaning fish.

Malibu sparked off several memories for the family over the years — the vanishing Boyles of course, and Angela's recognising Rod Steiger at the ice-cream freezer in the supermarket. For David a vivid memory was the unshakable grip of Helena's hand and, for that reason, the photograph snapped for them by an obliging fisherman of father and daughter hand-in-hand, with strained holiday smiles, on the Malibu pier, was the only American souvenir he took with him when he and Angela finally separated.

After Noumea

Recovering from his breakdown late that winter, Brian rented a weatherboard off-season holiday cottage at Palm Beach with two separate ocean views to guarantee serenity. A trailing edge of Cyclone Anna lashed his car as he drove up the peninsula, and on arrival he immediately lit a fire to keep the storm at bay and arranged himself in front of it. Below the cottage a high surf crashed on the beach. Eucalypt branches scraped along the roof guttering. Still tense from the drive he drank two brandies, cursorily read a magazine and went to bed.

Currawongs and kookaburras woke him early. The day was grey but fine, with a clear light. Right away he determined to make a schedule to live and work by. This took him the morning. Sharp at noon, as set out in his new schedule, he left for a walk down the gravel track through high trees to the beach.

Just around the first bend in the track he was ambushed by a blue heeler. Crouching low without barking, the dog ran around him to attack his legs from behind. Brian kicked out and it bit him on the calf though his jeans kept it from breaking the skin. He arrived at the beach still angry at the dog. Walking and jogging in alternate spurts, he became quickly puffed, his feet sinking into the soft sand. The storm had brought in dead fish and sea birds, plastic bottles, amorphous lumps of jelly from some marine invertebrate. Fine russet sand grains stuck to his feet and legs. Waves broke close inshore and a haze of moisture hung over the headland.

Returning to the cottage, breathing hard as he climbed the hill, he was again attacked by the dog. Furious, he yelled and ran wildly at it. The dog stood stunned at his reaction and then fled. From a safe distance it barked and showed its front teeth at him. Climbing the rock steps to the cottage he was surprised at how tense and angry it had made him.

At a table in the sunroom he attempted some cartoons immediately after lunch; snappy drawings with witty captions, nothing political. He tried out a few ideas, but none of them was satisfactory. As he discarded one cartoon after another, the kookaburras, sensing his presence in there, dived at the sunroom window and tapped their beaks on the glass until he threw them some crusts. They looked questioningly at him, as if he had thrown *their* schedule into disarray.

His concentration broken, Brian went out to forage for firewood on the hillside below the cottage. Most of the wood was still wet or too green to burn properly. Apathetically, he was snapping branches against his knee when a neighbour, out exercising her terrier, made an excuse for conversation.

'Collecting firewood, are you? That chimney doesn't draw, you know.'

Brian picked her at once as a nosy bourgeois person. She warned him of the grass ticks. 'A dab of ammonia'll get them off.'

Hovering around him she brought up the death the week before of his landlord's wife. Apparently the old woman's heart had given out while she was cleaning the kitchen for him, the new tenant.

'She was scrubbing out the oven when she went,' the neighbour said, peering at him intently. He felt she held him responsible. 'Yes, she's deady-bones,' she went on. He thought this was a little flippant. The neighbour had flushed middle-aged cheeks, with a drinker's broken veins. As he moved off she made him an offering of a piece of sodden gum branch.

He was too grateful. 'Oh, thank you very much,' he gushed, as if it were half a ton of dry mallee roots.

The cottage's holiday personality reflected that of its owner. The new widower was a retired surgeon in his seventies. Though clean, the cottage smelled of his pipes. *New Yorker* magazines lay about the living room and were piled in the wardrobes; other magazines seemed also to have been gathered up from his surgery waiting room over the years: fifteen-year-old copies of *Country Life* and the *Illustrated London News*. An old mantel radio sat on a bookshelf with pieces of driftwood, shells and sand-smoothed pebbles. The wide brick fireplace was smoke-stained up to its sandstone mantelpiece.

Whenever Brian stepped outside the kookaburras lined up optimistically, eight or nine abreast, along the verandah railing. Next in the pecking order came the magpies, then the currawongs, twisting their heads so their yellow set-back eyes caught every movement. He began to sketch the birds in charcoal but tired of it and threw the drawing away. Seen up close the kookaburras had interesting faces, with moist brown eyes like dogs, but sentimental nature-realism was not his area of interest.

The dead woman's summer clothes and straw handbags still hung in the cupboards. Her handwriting was on lists on a little bulletin board in the kitchen. 'Ring Mary Wednesday' said one note.

At night the cottage rocked in the wind, expanded and contracted in the temperature changes. Smoke from the occluded chimney hung in the rooms, making his eyes water, but he persevered with a fire each night, for the companionship. In the ceiling there were rattling footsteps, abrupt scamperings — presumably possums. Occasionally, waking with a start at some dark thuddings, Brian childishly suspected ghosts.

* * *

On his daily constitutional to the beach Brian began carrying a stick, slapping it on his thigh in a threatening manner as he rounded the bend near the blue heeler's home. The dog was also a confrontationist, continuing to rush him but keeping nimbly out of range of the stick. Though his heart beat loudly at each confrontation Brian refused to change his route or schedule. He began to think irrationally about the dog. These days he worried deeply about irrational thinking and took steady breaths to adjust his position. In bed, however, he lay considering methods of killing it. He favoured shooting it in the head at close range, in midlunge, with a large-bore pistol. Imagining this final collision, his head thudded furiously.

The nights were cold. Under a heap of blankets he lay listening to the surf booming and the wind sizzling through the eucalypts. His hair and pyjamas smelled of smoke.

Feeling lonely, Brian once or twice rang friends for conversation. But even while seeking affectionate noises and camaraderie he made tense cryptic remarks on the political situation and the human condition which made the recipients uneasy.

While on the telephone he doodled on a pad, drawing humorous faces, political likenesses — many aimless drawings. One of the faces he extended, adding limbs and a body. Then he had the figure, representing a right-wing politician he hated, force itself sexually on another celebrity whom he also detested. Brian drew ridiculously exaggerated genitals and a manic gleam in the rapist's eye. In life this politician was particularly expedient and a great upholder of the old moral values. On the victim's caricature he drew lush eyelashes and a pouting mouth. In reality this politician was vain and 'charismatic'. (Once at a party in Brian's hearing he had told a young woman whose waist he was holding: 'You could give me the anonymity I crave.' She took it as a compliment.)

Becoming more interested in his drawing than his conversation Brian said 'Mm' and 'Nn' and gradually the conversation lagged and came to an end.

When his ideas dried up he lay in the sunroom reading the retired surgeon's old *New Yorkers*. He pulled the curtains on the kookaburras' inquiring faces. None of the *New Yorker* cartoons made him laugh, though they were from his period. They had published five of his cartoons between 1967 and 1969, the best time of his life, when he was energetic, ambitious and game for anything.

His flushed-faced neighbour was in the habit of hanging around the dividing fence with her terrier. He believed she was prying while pretending to pick freesias and he endeavoured to ignore her. Strangely, she called to him briskly one morning and asked would he prevent his friends from 'hot-rodding' up the gravel track in their cars.

'No friends of mine have been here — in cars or otherwise,' he told her. Nevertheless he knew he looked immediately guilty. She said it turned the road into a quagmire when it rained. She said they weren't noisy partygivers up at Palm Beach. They liked a quiet life. She treated him with a falsely amiable condescension, as an unspecifiable interloper from the city. He wondered whether she was crazy.

Smiling fiercely, she then complained that his cat was digging up her garden, the naughty thing. She hoped it wouldn't destroy the local fauna, mentioning the beauty of the rosellas and the onrushing extinction of furry marsupials. She remembered when koalas clung to these very trees. She stressed upon him the delicate balance of nature.

A cat? He told her he didn't have a cat.

'It must be a stray,' she said with heavy sarcasm, turning and walking inside.

* * *

At nights he drank brandy, listened to the retired surgeon's radio and flipped through his paperbacks. Aimlessly drinking and pottering one night, he found a postcard in the writing desk — a sparkling summer photograph of Palm Beach.

For some reason he decided to send the postcard to his former lover, Anthea, with whom he was on dubious terms. Theirs had been an emotional, passionate relationship which had begun dramatically, caused pain, stabilised and then petered out. It had offered romance aplenty at the time. Anthea had inherited money and wanted to fulfil his dreams, to buy him a coastal hideaway like this one where he could work and they would swim and lie around scantily clad in the sun. They talked about the sea breeze filtering through net curtains onto their damp, after-love bodies. They made soft romantic plans and stayed in the hard city.

In truth he had let the offer pass, having then some perverse political set against accepting her largesse as well as an easy coastal life. Time together passed, three years. He could not pin it down but something had gone wrong. It had become an 'open' relationship. There had been a tacit understanding that this was the case, but not that it would be more 'open' for her than for him.

But Brian was feeling philosophical. More time had passed. Their first Christmas together he'd given her a book of his cartoons, dedicated to her. The dust jacket showed him sitting at his drawing board grinning ironically, as required of cartoonists, and wearing an Irish fisherman's sweater. Once she told him she was actually compelled to kiss his cover photograph, so truthfully had the photographer captured his likeness. The photographer, who hadn't received a credit, had been his wife when the photograph was taken, though not by the time the collection of cartoons was published.

Now he addressed the postcard to Anthea at the magazine where she worked. He began by selecting his words as carefully as the alcohol would allow, calling her Dear instead of Darling, but striking the right ironic yet affectionate note. He hoped she was well and happy; he mentioned where he was, that he was fit and accomplishing a lot of work. There was no obligation to reply, he added, hoping this little addition would ensure a reply.

He drew a small caricature of himself lying back on a beach. In his hand he drew a champagne glass and beside him, a magnum in an ice-bucket. In the air above the glass he drew little bubbles. He gave himself a smug grin and a pot belly. (In reality he was the thinnest he'd been.) He considered adding an amusing lewd touch to his bathing suit but decided against it. This time last year it would have struck the right note ('Thinking of you, as you can see!') but not now.

Thinking of her gave him an erection now, brought on anger and changed thought patterns. While considering how to sign off he wondered why he was sending it at all. Hadn't his last overtures been rebuffed? Trying to remember details of the occasion, how it happened, who had had the emotional upper hand, he was strangely imprecise on the surroundings. Perhaps a restaurant, Italian food, around the lowered tense voices.

The balance had somehow shifted. Something had tilted when she returned from a fashion assignment in Noumea. She had definitely had the emotional upper hand when last he saw her, he suddenly recalled. She had been alternately distant and sentimental, but an air barrier grew between them, choking him, until he fought clear. His heart began thumping. In the space at the bottom of the postcard he wrote: 'P.S. Why am I sending this? I must be mad!' and signed his initials.

He found a stamp in the desk, stuck it on the postcard and walked down to the mail box on the foreshore. In the dark he swung a cautionary stick but the dog must have been asleep and the wind in the eucalypts smothered his footsteps. He posted the card and returned.

74

Brian at once regretted sending Anthea the card. Pouring another brandy, he guessed he would be seen as grovelling to her. His tone had been too wheedling. Presumably she had another lover. He suspected the fashion photographer from the New Caledonia assignment. He could see her meeting him for drinks and laughing over fun times in Noumea. ('Oh, by the way, look at this strange postcard from Brian.') She would imply that their relationship had been dull and boring, that she had only been marking time. She would *dismiss* him.

Meanwhile, she would gain great emotional satisfaction from receiving the card and imagining the time he had spent thinking of her. Her ego would lap it up. She had always been spoilt. People coddled her too readily. Her politics were too apathetic and conservative. She was all style and no substance. Fashion photographers wore shirts unbuttoned to the waist and tight jeans. Brian felt like tearing out the mail box by the roots and smashing it open with a sledgehammer to retrieve his absurd postcard.

But now it was too late. Brian drank more brandy and traced its route: the postcard arrived at the post office, was sorted by mail workers, arrived in the magazine company's mailroom, was delivered by a teenager to Anthea's department, and finally landed in the in-tray on her desk. Her desk was apple-green. Numerous people besides her would peruse the postcard. There was no privacy in a postcard, he should have realised that. People felt compelled to trespass.

And his drawing style was recognisable. Until the trouble with management he had been a daily political cartoonist, an abrasive stylist with a faithful following of readers. Forty-six idealistic protesting letters had been sent to the editor when his cartoons abruptly ceased to appear. Most of the letter writers smelled censorship and some of them castigated the newspaper proprietor. All the letter writers were indignant — thirty-two were women. The editor had prevented any of the letters from being published, but when Brian left he had handed them to him with a smile of cynical goodwill.

'You might as well have these,' he said. 'Might do yourself some good with some of these pinko sheilas.'

Bad enough that his style was recognisable, his initials were also on the postcard. Snoopers would put two and two together and gossip about his low state. Media women were great annunciators of failure, especially career or heterosexual romantic failure. (Of homosexual romantic failure they were sweet and non-judgemental.) He was taking things badly, they would advise restaurants and cocktail parties. He would be filleted at Friday lunches and Saturday night dinners. Sending sentimental begging postcards to his former lover — how pathetic! Acquaintances would be momentarily delighted at the news. 'It's sad,' they would say, meaning 'delicious', coming on top of his acidic over-confidence and lack of objectivity.

For several days the postcard kept Brian in a depression. But he also worked out the time she would take to reply, making allowances for delivery delays, postal strikes, weekends. Every morning he watched for the postman; otherwise he kept to his schedule, striding down to the beach each noon for air and exercise. In anticipation of meeting the blue heeler his stomach tightened and his heart beat louder. Strangely, when the dog wasn't there he felt somehow cheated and tossed his stick into the bushes at the side of the track.

At the beach he now ran the full shore-length and back, about five kilometres. He persevered when the sand was soft and slushy and the shoreline too steeply inclined. He was anxious to establish mental and physical habits; health and stability seemed very necessary at the moment.

The table where he worked in the sunroom must have originated in his landlord's surgery. It was small and made of oak and he imagined it smelled of methylated spirits. He sat on a chair from the surgery waiting room, wondering how many sick and anxious people it had held over the years, how many of the damp-palmed patients clutching its arms were still alive. His pens were set out on his right and a pile of drawing pads on his left. He had a leather case of fine quality artists' and designers' pens and an Earl Grey tea tin holding brushes and a cigar box of coloured inks and tubes of paint. Back in his cross-hatching phase he had even favoured an ancient steel-nibbed pen and Indian ink, but for the past few years he had actually used nothing but cheap Japanese nylon-tipped throwaways.

Brian began a cartoon. Since his crack-up he had finished only four, including the postcard caricature of himself. Before he moved back to town he wanted to complete a folio of at least fifty, to have a solid log of work behind him, to re-establish himself. He was working away without inspiration when the telephone startled him. A woman's voice, neither young nor old, nasal and imperious, gave Anthea's name and asked whether she was there.

'Who is this?' he asked sharply, his pulse racing.

'Oh, this is a private call,' the woman said, and repeated her question.

'No, there's no one of that name here,' he replied.

The woman then asked, 'You know her, don't you?' Her voice had a drawling but insistent quality.

'We're acquaintances,' he said, stammering. 'What is your name?'

'That doesn't matter. Where can I find her?'

'I'm sure I don't know,' he said. When he hung up his hands were shaking.

Summer was in the humid beach air. As usual Brian jogged north along the shore. Suddenly he was jogging among nudes; naked men and women sauntered from the ocean, water streaming from their thighs and pubes. They were tanned all over yet until now they hadn't been there. Where had they come from? Two slender dark girls ran from the water and up the beach, the surface sand crust squeaking under their toes. Carefully Brian avoided their bouncing breasts, looking straight ahead. These people were very relaxed and flashed sociable smiles at one another but their nakedness had an air of potential umbrage about it.

Back in the sunroom he drew several more cartoons while a red wasp, frantically buzzing, died slowly on the window sill. It curled back on itself in agonies of frustration.

The postman's motorbike chugged up the track to the cottage between 9.15 and 9.30 each morning. From the sunroom window Brian watched for him, but when the postman stopped it was only to stuff the letterbox with magazine subscription invitations.

The blue heeler continued to rush at him with no loss of enthusiasm. He continued to thresh at it with his stick. Neither connected.

After his beach runs he lay on the sand thinking of Anthea. As the weather warmed, more cars began arriving from distant southern suburbs. He glanced among them for her car. It was easily recognisable: a white Alfetta, usually dented. She was a fast, aimless driver with a long record of traffic offences. The car was elsewhere.

The warmer evenings brought the mosquitoes out in force. He lowered the mosquito net over his bed and burned coils left by the dead woman. He kept a can of insect spray for tarantulas in the bathroom, funnel-webs in the laundry. Daily he upset the balance of nature. Nevertheless it thrived; bees hovered over the lavender bushes fringing the verandah, and butterflies flapped over the daisies and geraniums. In the fallen gum leaves lizards rustled.

Each morning at eight his florid neighbour rang a breakfast bell for the kookaburras. She threw them handfuls of chopped meat, assuming a most proprietary air, scolding and crooning. Brian felt she was trying to entice the birds away from his cottage, to keep them from his sinister city presence, to break up domicile patterns. So much for the balance of nature! She rang her little breakfast bell far too smugly for his liking.

He rose at six one morning. The kookaburras were already waiting patiently in the eucalypts around the cottage for their breakfast bell. He threw them special tasty chop tails, ham fat and bacon rinds until they were full and even the greedy currawongs and magpies had had enough. Through the sunroom window at eight he enjoyed watching them ignoring his neighbour's offerings. Shaking her head in surprise she went disconsolately inside.

Brian still had the letters protesting at his cartoons' departure from the newspaper. He spent a morning re-reading them. He'd regarded the editor's remarks as typically crass and cynical, but now he sorted the letters into male and female piles. From the female pile he eliminated those signed 'Mrs' or in a shaky elderly hand. This left sixteen which appeared to be from women who were in all likelihood idealistic and youngish. To these fans he now replied, writing identical chatty letters:

'Dear . . .,

'Thank you for your kind and generous support. It was gratifying, coming as it did during a trying time in my personal life and a worrying period in national affairs.

'Since I left the newspaper I have been living and working up at Palm Beach. It's marvellous what some sea air will do to restore the spirits. My old cottage has become a regular venue for jaded outcasts from the city. Please take this as an invitation to drop in for a drink if you are ever up this way. It would be a great pleasure to meet you.'

He gave his address and drew a little map showing the position of the cottage in relation to the main road.

One noon at the beach he saw a woman who may have been Anthea stooping to gather shells. Later, another Anthea was sunbathing nude. In each case his pulse quickened as he moved closer. Of course she could have changed her hairstyle, lost weight, got a suntan. He had to peer at each of them very closely before he realised she was not his lover.

At the north end of the beach nude swimming was now well established. Self-consciousness lessened as the weather grew still hotter. Brian began to recognise individual bodies as he jogged through the nudists each day.

Each day he still watched for the postman. There was no reply from Anthea, but the postman did bring a reply from one of the youngish idealistic female letter-to-the-editor writers. She explained that she was the 'co-ordinator' of a school for creatively gifted children in an inner-city suburb. The school had an Aboriginal name. She invited him to an 'open day' at the school next month. She knew this was imposing on him, but could he possibly donate twenty or thirty of his cartoons for auction on open day? The proceeds would go towards improving still further the school's cultural environment. The 'friends' of the school already included many leading figures in the world of the arts, and she was sure he would want to be included among them.

He threw the letter away.

The mosquitoes' aggression grew and the smell of burning mosquito coils pervaded the cottage. Brian was very restless and lacked the concentration for work. He found himself waiting for the publication day of Anthea's magazine, the first Wednesday of the month. On publication day he went down early to the village to buy a copy, to receive information about her.

At first he was struck by relief to see her byline on a fashion display which had been photographed on the island of Moorea. So she had travelled again recently, or not so recently — the magazine, though a monthly, was produced three months ahead. It was now November. She had been on Moorea perhaps in July.

The photographer also had a byline. Max Lang. Brian, a tremor in his chest, saw he was the same man who had accompanied her to New Caledonia. His photographs showed sleek models frolicking in turquoise lagoons, riding outriggers, slithering onto rafts. Tahitians gambolled democratically with them. Bare breasts were equally common on Polynesians and Caucasians. The photographs picked up the sheen of sweat on muscles, breasts and upper lips.

Brian looked beyond and around the edges of the photographs and clearly saw Anthea in a Tahitian print bikini directing these photographic sessions. She had a hibiscus in her hair and a drink waiting under the palms. She had a deep tan from nude sunbathing and laughed happily from behind big sun-glasses. She basked in the desire of rangy Club Med organisers and sulky Tahitian boys.

In the air space in front of the photographs he saw the photographer, Lang, clicking his camera. He was bare-chested, with a gold chain or two around his neck, a local necklace of shark teeth. He had a fashionable three-day beard growth. He was wiry, and brown from nude sunbathing. He was elegantly shabby and wore cut-off jeans and espadrilles in case of coral cuts. He pushed his sunglasses back on his wavy hair while he took pictures. He wiped spray from his lenses with a devil-may-care red bandanna. He had a drink waiting under the palms and the night planned.

Brian tossed the magazine aside and drank half a bottle of brandy. His temples pounded. He thought long and deeply about Anthea; at the same time he doodled with a nylon-tipped pen. Quick violent cartoons appeared: of carnal abandonment and mayhem involving people real and imaginary, sharks, deep-sea fish and cruel serrated objects. Anthea's body was the central motif. He drew it from memory, in fine detail, from many realistic angles, attempting to capture filmy textures, velvety anterior and ventral tissues and tiny blemishes he had once caressed. He brought out his old steel-nibbed pen, his full range of pencils. Representations of Anthea filled his drawing pads; her face peered at him from a dozen angles. Brian's mind was fired with energy. His pen raced over the paper until it ran dry, and he grabbed up another. He drew his savage cartoons until he heard the kookaburras tapping their beaks on the verandah rail at dawn. His eyes suddenly burned with fatigue and he collapsed on the sunroom divan.

When he woke at noon he remembered past misty progressions of time in a new sequence and with abrupt clarity. The cartoons disturbed him more than he thought possible. He stumbled down the track to the beach. In the humidity the dog chose to ignore him. The beach was baking and crowded. Trudging through the sand fully dressed, he stared into the faces of naked women and muttered her name. Private tears shot from his eyes. Acting on the complaints of their wives and girlfriends four men bustled him from the beach. They pushed him fiercely towards the road but his demeanour turned away overt violence and they merely swore at him and shook their heads. On his hazy way home the dog rushed him. He flapped haphazardly at it and it tore his calf.

In the sunroom he placed the cartoons in his folio of work accomplished, then locked the door and kept out of the room. Now he stayed indoors all the time, opening the front door only to feed the birds, and trying not to think of the cartoons or the images they represented. In another moment of clarity a few days later, however, he burned them in case the authorities, in possession of his postcard to Anthea, should want to speak to him again and came up the peninsula to continue their inquiries.

The View
from the Sandhills

I'm admitting it, I've seen some great tits and some of the bushiest boxes you could imagine on the sly. Speaking of which I saw that Anne Lang from that Channel 9 current affairs show's tits this close last summer. She was arguing with a bloke, skinny, looked like a poofter to me, and they walked past me in the sandhills with her knockers swinging away without noticing me.

I do like a big tit, I must say. I make no apologies on that score. All these skinny modern chicks with their perky threepenny bits do nothing for me. I suppose you'll read something into that but I'm old-fashioned that way. And I do like a big nipple, brown for preference, something with a bit of suck in it. I'm not fussy, I don't mind a bit of droop, not if they're worth drooping, but once the sag sets in, finito. Give me your forty-year-old who's looked after herself any day and you can keep your teenagers. I saw a woman once, a dago, with the biggest brownest nipples you've ever seen. I was still inside then, watching TV, the ethnic station, Channel 0, by accident one night. This woman was getting into bed with some wog shepherd up in the mountains and her tits nearly filled his wooden hut. The word spread like wildfire and next night every set in the jail's on Channel 0. Everyone passed up those rootable girls on *Dallas* and Channel 0 turned out to be a desert of no tits, no English — just a screen full of Yugoslav jugglers!

I wrote to Anne up at Channel 9 and mentioned I'd seen her at the beach, enclosing a snap of her for proof, and trusted she was

OK, what with her crying that day and everything, but I didn't get a reply. Your boyfriend looked a right animal, I said, and doesn't deserve someone with your figure and ability. Looks aren't everything in men, I said, something I learned in jail. I mentioned that with her mature bustline, if she'd excuse the expression, and ample curves, she'd be better off getting into films and not wasting her career on those television homosexuals. My advice is you need a real man, I said, if you don't mind me saying so, and I went on in that vein for a bit, mentioning a few legendary blokes I knew inside over the years and what they used to get up to.

I've seen many a strange sight at the beach. Many's the fuck I've snapped over the years, though they've dropped off lately since nudism's become popular. All doing it at home these days I reckon. 'Excuse me, Mum, the boyfriend and I are toddling upstairs for a quickie.' They're shameless, these young chickies, suck off anyone right off the street and not turn a hair. When I first got out it did surprise me that even Catholic women say 'shit' these days, but, no, brazen women don't upset me. Quite the contrary. I'm dead against mock modesty. Women used to stand on their dignity too much, don't I know it!

You have to get there early or all the good spots are taken. The same dozen or so turn up most days. I reckon about fifty per cent are there to see the men. We women-lovers are a dying breed, the whole world's turning poofter. And lesbian. You'd be surprised at the amount of twat tickling that goes on any warm day. I see a couple of girls come out of the surf away from the main beach holding hands and frolicsome and I think, hullo! Here we go! First they dry themselves, then surprise, surprise, they need some suntan cream applied. Don't forget all those vulnerable little nooks and crannies! By the time they've oiled each other they're so steamed up, kissing and going down on it they don't even notice me, not even standing up, not even once when I came twice not thirty yards from them. I think it's something in the sun does it to them.

I get the 8.15 bus from the station and I'm on the beach by nine. I usually take my camera and a good pair of Jap binoculars, a bit of lunch, a magazine and a couple of those little cardboard packs of Milo with the drinking straw attached. One of the new-fangled things I do like since I got out is the way they have these little cardboard packs of juice and what-have-you that you stack in the fridge. Even Milo now. I like my Milo. Before I went inside it only came in those green tins with a bloke carrying a bull on his back. Milo was hard to get inside. Plenty of tea full of pieces of twig and hessian bag and horse shit for all I know, and a jar of Nescafé if you buy it with your laundry wage, but Milo, no. I whack all this in a plastic bag and I'm off for the day.

As you'd expect, when I first got out I was all over the place like a mad woman's lunchbox. Sex on my mind the whole time, racing from one beach to another, must have trudged over every sandhill in the state! Now I mostly concentrate on the one beach. Don't think I'm going to give the beach away! They've got these sort of vigilante groups now and they come at you all fury and saggy balls, not even stopping to put their pants on, with the intention of beating the shit out of you. They really get them in a knot. A few times I ran for it but I got wise in my old age. Now if they see the sun glinting off the binoculars and scramble up the sandhills after me, by the time they get to me I'm reading my *TV Week*, sipping my Milo.

'What're you doing, you bloody pervert?' they say. Insults don't hurt me in the slightest. 'I beg your pardon, mate,' I say. 'I beg your pardon.' I act a bit put out but not aggressive. If you stand on your dignity people lose their nerve and shuffle around. It's hard to be belligerent with no pants on. After a while they go back to their volleyball. Once, just to be cheeky, I took a snap of them all stomping away, all those indignant arses wobbling down the hill. I look at it sometimes for a laugh.

Never show weakness. I learned that inside. Lesson Number One. Stay wary for trouble, yes. Pretend ignorance of everything that's going on, certainly. But never show weakness or you'll have more cocks up you than Dora on pay night.

There's another lesson, one I taught myself. Live inside your head. It's stood me in good stead. Now I'm philosophical about interruptions. Get a good fantasy going and you can always start again. Keep the memory for later, that's what I've developed. I've developed a photographic memory of women's bodies.

Remember that TV commercial where this woman comes in after a hard game of tennis? Brunette mature type, glowing with perspiration, moist forehead and upper lip? She takes the sweat-band off her head and walks into her bathroom talking loudly to no one like they all do, shrugging self-consciously about being hot and sweaty.

But with a little knowing smile. Do I know that smile! Well, she steps cleverly out of her clothes and into the shower so you can't see anything, and next thing she's standing in the bathroom with a yellow towel wound tightly round her tits, her wet hair slicked back, rubbing deodorant into her ultra-smooth armpits.

Believe me that I can fill in the gap between her giving that little smile and when she's all spick and span and wrapped up in her towel. Actually, I keep her in the little tennis frock a bit longer than when she's on TV, and ask her to keep her sandshoes on.

When she comes into the bathroom her sandshoes make little squeaky sounds on the floor. Dianne likes to bend over the wash-basin and splash water on her hot face and I come up behind her and pull down her frilly tennis pants. Even though she acts surprised at me being in the bathroom, Dianne's all hot and moist from the tennis and I go right up her, a tit in each hand.

She's desperate for me as it turns out. The bathroom is gleaming, very modern, gold taps and big soft towels everywhere. Dianne is so impressed she pleads for another one right away. We generally sink onto a heap of soft towels with Dianne moaning for me. Her thighs are tanned and strong from all that tennis but my superior strength never fails to amaze her. We're both insatiable — her husband's a stockbroker or lawyer or something who doesn't give her much — so we have another one in the shower after Dianne's gobbled me and I've spent a lot of time soaping and sucking her big nipples.

But unfortunately time's getting on. Dianne's got a big dinner party to organise for the Liberal Party and the children to be picked up from private schools. She wraps the yellow towel around her, kisses me sadly goodbye and I leave the mansion by the back door. *C'est la vie.* I'm not jealous of anyone in this world. I could've been a lawyer or doctor myself if I'd put my mind to it. My mother maintained that it was the Depression that kicked me off on the wrong track. I thought a lot of her. The last time she didn't want me to leave jail so I didn't pursue it. One day she came to see me out at Long Bay. 'How long have you been in altogether, Paddy?' she asked me. I told her twenty-three years. 'What a wasted life,' she said.

You would have heard that it was only when she died that I tried to get out, put my case to the Parole Board. It might sound funny but when she said I'd better stay in for the good of the family I went along with it. I could've got out years ago but it was my way of paying her back for causing her all that trouble. When my mother was dying she told my sister, 'Paddy did a lot of bad things and a lot of good things. Paddy could've been better.' She had a very strong personality.

On the matter of my urges, as you put it, one day a few weeks ago I decided to get a bit closer for once. I surprised myself. Take it in easy stages, I advised myself. I wandered down to Tamarama beach from the boarding house and just got in amongst all the bare tits, bold as brass. I just walked in among all the girls and sat down. It's only topless, not nude, mind you, they wear these little skimpy strips of cloth barely covering their cracks, but you can imagine the rest. I lay there so close I could've reached out in any direction and just grabbed a nork. I was relaxed but nervy, if you know what I mean.

But it got me going, I can tell you, those plump bodies gleaming with suntan oil, that sweet coconut smell, it was heaven. I like to crack a nice fat in public, the sun beating down and all, roll my bathers right down to my stalk and think away, get a bit of a throb going. Look Mum, no hands! I was teasing myself thinking I could just lean over and fasten onto a nearby tit or tweak a bunch of that pubic hair they don't mind flashing. Except probably the girl wouldn't even blink. Up close their faces are pretty but vacant, all thinking of being fucked rotten, but half of them wouldn't know if you were up them with an armful of cane chairs, as the saying goes. You could be in, out, and in bed with a good book before they finished their ice-creams.

Anyway, these two young sluts started giggling at me, taking the piss, so I got up and left. Fifteen or so and tits no bigger than mine, in any case. No sweat. That's women all over. They didn't worry me, but why stress myself is how I look at it. There's no hurry.

I've looked after myself. Lean but wiry, my mother used to say. I exercise every day, take vitamins and that ginseng stuff for vitality. My sort of olive skin takes a good tan so I wear shorts all year round. I eat plain food, lots of yoghurt, and I always keep a couple of those health bars in my pocket. A woman I used to write to in Long Bay said I had a very trim physique for a man my age. She admired my sensitive fingers. Surgeon's hands, she said. She was an official jail visitor, not bad looking, blonde, fortyish, spoke in a flirty broad way. I took her words for gospel and wrote back that I wouldn't mind sticking those surgeon's hands right up. Surprise, surprise, the superintendent gets the letter and I do an extra two years.

C'est la vie. I wouldn't mind seeing *her* down at the beach one lonely night, snatch like a clam, I'd reckon. I've kept the address but I'm not stupid. They'd trace it to me. Perhaps a few random phone calls, hankie over the phone and some hot suggestions just to juice her up. That was a joke, that's never been my scene. All my ones have asked for it, you can look it up in the evidence. Anyway, that's all in the past and it's no use crying over spilt milk.

You'd understand that I wasn't programmed to do a crime of a violent nature. It's not something I can figure out. It's odd but these things happen. The remarks got to me, sure, the jibes, but it was the screaming made me go black and when she fell she hit her temple and it bled a lot. It was more an accident.

I keep getting the feeling you think I have trouble relating to women. Well you can scotch that one. Actually I'm thinking very seriously of going up the north coast and getting a partner to live with me. Getting a shack near the sea, doing a spot of fishing. I hear you can get an island girl to do your washing, cooking and so on for six bob a week. That'd suit me, grass skirt and bare tits. I sometimes wonder about my wife, where she is. She was only twenty-one when she left. She would never divorce me, being a Catholic. I could see us living together up the coast. I dream of her, our year together. I think of heaven sometimes. Funny, imagining her as a mature middle-aged woman.

Sweetlip

I am outlining the inquiries I have made since speaking to you after the cremation service.

As Director of Security for P & M may I suggest this report be kept confidential, perhaps restricted to the Board of Directors.

Many remarks recorded here, especially some by the family, were either hearsay or pure emotional supposition. There could be legal and other worries for us in their circulation. The resort is, of course, part of the Dunbar Group of companies, of whom we are more than aware in the present takeover climate.

I leave this aspect to you. By detailing the events chronologically I hope you will have a clearer picture of this affair which has distressed all of us in the Company.

On Saturday, 22 November last year, ten P & M executives arrived by North Queensland Airways Sikorsky helicopter on Sweetlip Island, the venue for the Company's annual sales and marketing conference. Following Company safety policy of staggering our executives' flights, another eight arrived next day, and the final six on Monday.

As Managing Director, Rex Lang, one of the first arrivals, headed the twenty-four-man party. He was joint chairman of the working parties with Kevin Brownbill, Manager of the Services' Division.

Their convention agenda was full. From Sunday until Friday —

with Wednesday a lay day for a fishing cruise — they assembled each morning at 8.30 in the Marlin Hotel's conference room. They worked, with meal and coffee breaks, until 5.00 p.m.

However, that still left time for rest and recreation. Each morning some exercised before work. For example, Brownbill kept up his jogging. Lang would go for a walk along the lagoon, then swim before breakfast, his custom for the past twenty years.

Some of the party apparently nursed hangovers. No names are forthcoming here. There are six bars on Sweetlip Island, including one disco, 'Randy's', which remains open till 4.00 a.m. It would be perhaps unreasonable not to expect that at night some of the party discussed sales and marketing strategy in some of them.

One who touched hardly a drop of alcohol, however, was Rex Lang. He had decided to spend a 'dry' convention week in order to lose some weight.

It goes without saying he was not an habitué of 'Randy's'.

He resisted his colleagues' teasing. On Tuesday, 25 November, he sent a postcard to his wife (I report this with Mrs Janice Lang's permission), saying 'Darling, here I am in a little beach hut, just like that holiday on Maui in '73. Great weather, feeling fine. The only way to work! Starting Day 3 — still no booze! See you Sunday. Love, Rex.'

As for the food question, the Sweetlip Island brochures say, 'Eat, drink and be merry.' The guests can be expected to comply. Each week there is a South Sea Island Night where the guests feast on pigs cooked in the traditional Polynesian manner on hot stones. There is also an Oriental Night, a Roaring Twenties Night, a Left Bank Night and a King Neptune Night, with the menu varying accordingly. Lunch is a variety of hot fish and meat dishes or a 'mouth-watering smorgasbord served from a real Pacific Island canoe'.

The local reef fish form a staple part of the resort diet.

Rex Lang marked with a cross on the postcard where his 'beach hut' was located. It was actually No. 1 in the Frangipani Lodge, at $103.50 a day among the most expensive accommodation on the island. Facing the lagoon, and almost out of range of the demands of the public address system, it was also the farthest cabin from the resort complex.

The first member of the party to become ill was Derek James from Perth. He reported 'an upset stomach and diarrhoea' on Monday morning. On Tuesday he was joined on the sick-list by Dick Scrutton from the Sydney office, suffering from 'a swelling on the face'. Hugh Gillam from Adelaide also complained of 'stomach pains'.

The convention continued, in its relaxed way, with Rex Lang chairing most of Tuesday's meetings. After some indecision about tides and weather the party spent Wednesday cruising the Barrier Reef, bottom-fishing for sweetlip, coral trout, red emperor and groper.

Nigel Donnelly from Sydney was the next to report sick, experiencing 'sea-sickness and diarrhoea' an hour after departure. His illness paled, however, beside that of Ian McPhee, the Perth sales manager.

He recalled, 'We set off on a launch around the outer islands. I had been off-colour the night before, but I became much worse, with severe vomiting and stomach cramps. The spasms got worse and worse until I was paralysed down my left side. The others thought I'd had a stroke or coronary.'

McPhee was put aboard a sea-plane which flew him back to Sweetlip. There the resident nurse gave him a pethidine injection and he was transferred by boat to the mainland and then by ambulance to Petersen Hospital.

'The matron gave me another needle,' McPhee reported, 'and

this quietened me down. The doctor gave me an electro-cardiogram test and said my heart was OK — it was food poisoning. They kept me in hospital overnight and I spent the rest of my time on Sweetlip in bed.'

The Petersen Hospital records have McPhee admitted for 'gastritis' on the twenty-sixth and discharged the next day.

(According to Personnel, McPhee is fifty-three. He was last hospitalised three years ago for a hernia operation. Further promotion is not envisaged.)

On Thursday, while McPhee was recuperating, the conference continued. That night there was a jolly atmosphere at dinner. Brownbill and Lang, sitting together, chose the same main course, beef tournedos, and had a friendly argument over the wine Brownbill had ordered.

Lang, in his sixth day of abstinence, laughingly bolstered his argument by tasting and swallowing a mouthful of Brownbill's wine, a Lindeman's 1963 Hunter River burgundy.

He drank no more wine. In good spirits he left the dining room at 9.30 and went to his cabin.

The sixth Company man to become sick was Peter L'Estrange of Melbourne. He succumbed to 'an attack of vomiting and diarrhoea' in the early hours of Friday, 28 November, which was to last the whole day. In the hubbub of that morning, however, his troubles were ignored.

When the conference assembled at 8.30 a.m. three men were missing: McPhee, still recovering from the illness which precipitated the air-and-sea mercy dash, L'Estrange, then in the middle of his gastric attack, and Lang.

At 9.15 a.m. Brownbill sent one of the Sydney team, Jim Beech, to Lang's cabin to see if he had over-slept. Beech knocked on the door, received no answer and walked around to the lagoon side of the cabin and peered through the window.

Beech reported later; 'I noticed the bathroom light on, vomit on top of the bed and Rex's wallet and pens on his desk top. I hurried back and told Kevin Brownbill.'

Brownbill obtained the key to Lang's room and opened the door. He saw vomit on the bed and remembers seeing two silver pens, a watch and a wallet on the bedside table.

'I found Rex lying face up on the bathroom floor. He was naked, with a wash cloth covering his genitals. I rushed to get the nurse. When she examined him she said, "He's dead."'

I travelled up to her home at Whale Beach to interview Mrs Janice Lang on 9 December, 15 January and 23 January. She was obviously under much stress and increasingly anxious to see the matter resolved. Here I must say that her emotional state was heightened by the presence of her stepson, Max Lang, on the first occasion. He appeared especially tense and fatigued by events, to the extent of making unnecessary legal threats against the Company.

Mrs Lang remembers the morning of Friday, the twenty-eighth, with great clarity. 'It was 11.15. As soon as I saw the Chairman get out of his car I knew something had happened to Rex. It's amazing how you behave at a time like that. I found myself acting the perfect hostess. I heard myself ask, "Would you like a drink?" I got out the gin and tonic in a dream.'

According to Mrs Lang, a Constable Grundy telephoned her from Sweetlip at 11.30. 'He told me the police were taking Rex's body to the mainland, to the town of Petersen, for an autopsy and that they'd let me know the results in three weeks. He volunteered, "It's not food poisoning — he wasn't dehydrated." He repeated that four times. He said, "You realise we may never know what killed him."'

✻ ✻ ✻

Four days later the body arrived in Sydney with permission from the local coroner for cremation.

'I saw him at the funeral parlour,' she said, 'just to make sure he was dead. I was surprised. He looked wonderful, so marvellously fit and sun-tanned from the island.'

The funeral service and cremation were performed.

Rex Lang was sixty-two.

As you will see later, cremation seems to have been a mistake.

For chronology's sake I insert two occurrences here without comment. When Lang's belongings were returned to his widow his two silver Parker pens, one a ballpoint, the other a fountain pen, each with the initials R.W.L., were not among them.

Six days after his death an elderly kitchen hand on Sweetlip Island, Tom Eden, died suddenly after a big meal of coral trout and tiger prawns.

When, almost two months later, Mrs Lang had still not received any autopsy results from the police, she phoned the Petersen coroner. He said he had never heard of her husband and had no record of him.

'I am being stone-walled,' she told me the next day. 'A great wall of silence comes down when I ask why my husband died.'

I travelled up to Petersen on 9 February, accompanied, on his insistence, against my wishes and with the Chairman's approval, by Max Lang.

Time has stood still at 1955 in Petersen — that must be understood by the Company in any of our dealings with the town and the district. The people are predominantly cane farmers and fishermen though tourism is becoming the main money earner. The green and white chimneys of the Petersen Sugar Cane

Co-operative dominate the skyline, the pace is slow and the main event in town during our visit was the Petersen Live Theatre's presentation of *Hello, Dolly* at the Alhambra Theatre.

I learned that the Lang post mortem had been performed at Egerton, fifty kilometres north, by a local G.P., a Dr Reginald Davies. He was agitated at our appearance in his surgery and assumed the full dignity of the provincial medical practitioner.

'I am most annoyed at being asked about this. I just performed the autopsy,' he said. 'Let's leave matters in the hands of the proper officials.'

'So much for professional compassion,' Max interposed.

The doctor looked furious but controlled himself sufficiently to say he would average one post mortem examination a year. He had performed this one on the sudden absence of the resident medical officer down the coast. He had suspected a heart attack in the beginning, but after conducting several tests had found the heart 'OK'. He had not been told before the autopsy about food poisoning on Sweetlip Island.

He would expect any food poisoning sickness in Lang's case to be more prolonged, with attendant dehydration.

'This man was not dehydrated,' he said. 'Apart from a fatty liver he appeared in good physical condition for a man his age.'

'Your father liked a drink, did he?' he asked Max, rather unnecessarily.

He could find nothing to establish the cause of death so he had declined to issue a death certificate.

He had taken samples of the heart, lung, liver, kidneys, blood, and stomach contents. He had handed the specimens to Constable Grundy, suggesting he freeze them before sending them down to the State Pathology Laboratory in Brisbane for testing.

Some time after this transferral some of the organ samples disappeared. One was the heart.

✻ ✻ ✻

This situation was revealed in a telephone conversation immediately afterward with the Chief Pathologist in Brisbane. He reported that he had received specimens of liver and kidney only, and then not until three weeks after the post mortem.

Unfortunately they had been frozen instead of being sent in formalin. Freezing had altered the tissue structure and rendered the histological results useless. As a matter of fact the freezing process itself had been bungled, the organs having been allowed to thaw.

'They look as if they might have come down here in the back of a car,' said the pathologist. 'This is summer we're talking about. This is the tropics. Do I need to spell it out?'

No request had been made for a food poisoning test, and no stomach contents had been received in any case. 'What we'd be looking for here would be bacteriological infective staphylococci clostrida. Therefore we'd need to study the intestinal contents for bacteria, culture growth and so forth.'

I discovered that Mrs Lang had also contacted the Chief Pathologist. He said he told her 'We have no heart specimen and I believe it was never sent.'

These people are extraordinary in their lack of subtlety. Then he told her he had written to the police to check if the heart was 'lying around somewhere'.

He told me he had no evidence to show the cause of death.

The symbolism of the missing heart affected Max Lang. There was a scene that night with a drink waiter in the dining room of the Aloha Motor Inn in Petersen which did the reputation of P & M no credit at all.

Max's antagonistic attitude carried over next day into our meeting with the policeman who had first taken his father's body from the island to the mainland and had then been entrusted with

101

the organ samples. Constable Donald Grundy, a heavy-set, officious young man, was extremely defensive about his role in the affair.

'Where is my father's heart?' Max began.

'I couldn't comment on that. A court hearing is pending,' said the constable.

'What about the other missing autopsy specimens?'

'I couldn't comment, I said. Listen, I don't have to talk to you people. This is all *sub judice*.'

I said, 'There was at least one case of food poisoning of another of the P & M party the same week as Mr Lang died, but I believe you insist he didn't die from food poisoning?'

'There is always dehydration with food poisoning and Lang wasn't dehydrated.'

At this stage Max asked Grundy brusquely, 'Who knocked off my father's pens?'

'You're upset about the missing pens, but I didn't see any pens in the room. I made a list of the valuables in my book. See, there's no pens on the list. The island management checked the list and signed my book. I even sent his valuables down to Mrs Lang at my own cost to do the right thing. The police force doesn't pay for those things.'

Max returned to the attack. 'You're covering up. What did you do with the body samples?'

Grundy was barely controlling himself. 'There's no cover-up. I do my report and send it to my boss, the district inspector. He reads it and sends it to the Coroner, who sets a date for the hearing.'

There was no stopping Max. 'You were the last person to have all my father's body samples. What did you do with them?' He was becoming hysterical. 'Where did you freeze them? In your bloody kitchen fridge? There are lots of implications there, constable. I suppose your fucking cat ate them!'

102

The station sergeant said either we left or he would lock Max up.

Our conversation with Barry McGlynn, who is Clerk of the Court and Registrar as well as Coroner at Petersen, was less tense but equally circuitous. A certain Alice in Wonderland aspect began to enter the investigation at this point.

'When will the Lang inquest be held?' I asked him.

'We don't have a date. We're waiting for the files to come back.'

'From where?'

'From where they've been.'

'Where's that?'

'You better ask the police. It's just a matter of hoping the damn things come back.'

At this stage I switched tack. 'When did you know that parts of the body were missing?'

'Not till some time later when we started checking up. If they are lost, that is. That's what the files are away for.'

'Why did you give the OK for cremation even though the specimens were lost?'

'I didn't have a clue anything was missing when I approved the cremation. I didn't have a clue in the wide world that parts were missing.'

'How were the specimens lost?'

'I wouldn't have a clue. You'd better ask the police.'

'What is the normal procedure in cases of sudden death where specimens are taken for testing? Was this procedure followed?'

'The procedure is for the police to arrange for the specimens to go to the State Pathology Laboratory. I don't know whether this or that happened or what happened.'

Max had been quiet until then. 'Where were the specimens frozen?' he asked.

The Coroner said, 'I couldn't help you there.'

103

'There must be a policy,' Max shouted. 'Are they frozen in the hospital, the police station, a domestic refrigerator?'

'Goodness knows.'

Max and I booked in overnight at the Marlin Hotel on Sweetlip Island. We took the helicopter across from the mainland and checked in to two cabins in Frangipani Lodge, Nos 3 and 4. The staff, presumably tipped off about us from the mainland, were cool but efficient.

I asked Max to allow me to question people alone, not wishing any emotional outburst to jeopardise our position. He agreed, though unwillingly, busying himself taking photographs from all angles of Cabin No. 1 where his father had died.

The bar staff, cocky and talkative earlier, were nervous when I introduced myself over a glass of beer. The bar manager announced in a loud voice, 'We haven't heard anything about people getting food poisoning. No one we know has been sick. That goes for all my staff.'

The nursing sister who examined Lang's body, Rhonda Lynch, was slightly more forthcoming. 'I don't know what was the cause of death,' she said. 'The other man in the party who was taken to Petersen Hospital was diagnosed as suffering from food poisoning.' This statement was volunteered without prompting.

'Sometimes people on holidays eat and drink more than usual,' she added, 'and food they're not used to.'

I asked her if she entered in her medical records every case she treated.

'Yes.'

'Could I see your treatment records for November-December?'

'That wouldn't be ethical. All records of illness must be kept confidential.'

I asked whether an island employee, Tom Eden, had died shortly after Lang, perhaps from food poisoning.

She said he was an old fat man who had died in his sleep.

The nurse did direct me to a friend of Tom Eden's, Murray Burns, an elderly carpenter.

I said, 'Murray, I understand you were a mate of Tom's?'

'Yes, for nineteen years. Our huts were next to each other. I had to ask the boss for a move to another hut. I couldn't stand being so close to where Tom died.'

I said, 'I had a mate who died here the week before Tom. I wondered if they both died from the same cause.'

'Tom died in his sleep. He was laying on his bed. It was his day off. I didn't see him around in the morning so I went next door and there he was. At least he died peacefully in his sleep. I reckon what killed him was rolling around those 44-gallon drums of garbage in this temperature.'

'Did he smoke?'

'No, but he was a big eater and liked his drink. He was a very big man. He wouldn't have much for breakfast, but he'd make up for it later. Like one night he said he felt like eggs. He cooked ten eggs and sat down and ate the lot. He'd eat steak for tea and follow it up with a plate of fish.'

'Did he always do his own cooking?'

'Yes. Poor Tom. He was going to retire in January too.'

Alex Stack, the manager of Sweetlip Island, is a tall suave man whose clothing and accoutrements proclaim his occupation as a resort manager. He was not pleased to see me and managed to mention the several links between P & M and the Dunbar group.

'You would be better talking to the police,' he said. 'Look, I went down to Mr Lang's room with the nurse and saw he was dead. He was lying on his back on the bathroom floor with his head near the toilet. He was undressed, with a wash cloth covering his thighs. He had been sick in the room. There was a mess in the bed, some vomit, a small amount of faeces. I left the nurse there and rang the police on the mainland. We got a policeman over in the helicopter and he took the body away.'

'What about his belongings?'

'We made a list of the valuables. The policeman rang a week later and asked if I had noticed any silver pens in the room, because the family were complaining they were missing. I said no. Who would steal pens with someone's initials on them? It's ridiculous.'

Asked whether any other people were ill during the week of the fatality, Stack answered, 'Yes, during their fishing trip one got very seasick and had to be taken to hospital.'

Presumably it would have been devastating for business if a food poisoning story had broken just before the main holiday season?

He became very peeved at the mention of food poisoning. 'Any talk about us covering up an epidemic is nonsense. With hundreds of guests you'd expect a couple to get upset stomachs. The way some of them eat and drink it's no wonder!'

I said any epidemic would surely show up in the medical records. That would be one way of settling it. Could I see those records?

'They're confidential. Medical ethics and so on.'

Would he be happy to give evidence at an inquest?

'I have no more to tell.' Stack shrugged. 'Someone dies . . .'

Miscellaneous points:

There is a fish poison called ciguatera to be found in the flesh of a wide range of Barrier Reef fish, including some of the most edible species such as sweetlip, coral trout, red bass, red emperor and groper. Most doctors would be unfamiliar with the symptoms of ciguatera poisoning.

Sweetlip Island had trouble with contaminated water supplies in 1974, 1977 and 1979.

The island does not slaughter its own meat. This is done at

Egerton and the frozen carcases are brought across to Sweetlip by boat. The resort's food handling conditions are checked periodically by State health authorities. No prosecutions have ever ensued.

Since the Lang episode any dead body is flown to Egerton instead of Petersen. A more obliging G.P. now signs the death certificates.

McPhee, the Petersen Hospital patient, says he has still not recovered from the 'seasickness', as Stack termed it, three months later. (His sales figures for February are down 11.5 per cent.)

Mrs Lang says she could no longer disregard foul play. (I refer directors to the third paragraph of this report.)

Mrs Lang reports: 'I get more suspicious of everyone the longer this drags on. I don't know what to think. Was there some fish sting on his body? Did he choke on his vomit? Did he have a stroke? Who knows now? Would someone have benefited from his death? It's so humiliating and depressing for me. I can't get a death certificate so I can't get probate granted. Society needs a cause of death.'

(She has one point of course in that even with an open finding or death-unknown decision she can't get life insurance and her compensation from us is affected. If she can't get an inquest she can't get to first base.)

The police at least could be in a position of censure for their handling of the organ samples. Do we push this?

Directors should be reminded that P & M has two potential and vigorous antagonists here: the Dunbar Group and the Queensland Government.

Because of all the circumstances my feeling is that it will not be possible to obtain a definite cause of death from any coroner's inquiry. In the meantime these are my recommendations:
- We should get statutory declarations from all P & M people

mentioned in this report, including full details of their illnesses, last meal eaten, etc.

- We need full details of McPhee's hospitalisation, treatment and diagnosis. A letter of authority from him to the hospital is necessary.

- We should have a written report from Lang's own doctor covering his last health check, plus his opinion on the possible cause of death.

- Most importantly, we must satisfy ourselves that everything is handled at an inquiry from 'our' point of view. This can only be done by engaging legal counsel away from either Petersen or Egerton. These small-town networks are amazing. We should subtly seek a different town for the inquest venue.

Max Lang has asked that our legal people press the police and the island management about the positioning of his father's body. He seems to find it peculiar, its neatness on the bathroom floor, particularly the washcloth covering the groin area.

I quote him without comment: 'Dad was not a modest man, he was not prissy. If he was dying the last thing he'd worry about would be "decency".' He added, rather unnecessarily, 'We were brought up to regard nudity as quite natural. We swam nude when we could. At home Dad did the gardening with just an old piece of sack tied round his waist. He was a scallywag.'

For the record, Max also became sick on the island. He phoned me from his cabin at 9.00 a.m. after our overnight stay. He said he had been vomiting and defecating most of the night. He seemed in a bad way. I took him to the nurse, who injected him with something to quieten his stomach spasms. Though pale and weak he was recovering by the time we took off in the helicopter at 3.00 p.m., and slept in the plane all the way down the coast.

The cause of his illness is not known. My own view, for what it is worth, is that it was precipitated by his drinking until 2.00 a.m. at 'Randy's'.

The Bodysurfers

The murders took the gloss off it. Crossing over the Hawkesbury, David began thinking of them, anticipating the bridge over Mooney Mooney Creek they would soon cross, the picnic area below where, he had read in the papers, the lovers had apparently been forced from their car two nights before, ordered to strip and then struck and run over repeatedly by the murderer's car. When David finally drove over the bridge and the station wagon rounded the bend past the murder site, he nudged Lydia and pointed it out but said nothing because of the younger kids. He thought he could see deep savage skid marks in the gravel.

They were heading this Friday evening for the weekend shack David had just bought at Pearl Beach; he, Lydia, and his children Paul, Helena and Tim. Having turned over the house at Mosman to his wife since their separation, David now lived nearer town in a flat with a green view of Cooper Park. He missed the water in his windows, however the dependable harbour glimpses framed by the voluptuous pink branches of his own plump gum tree, as well as the early morning bird calls, the barbecue, the irresistible nationalistic combination of bush and water, so he decided that at last he would buy a weekend shack on the coast.

'I see no reason why we can't get what we want,' he had remarked to Lydia, his new lover, as romantic in these matters as himself. He knew exactly what he was looking for. It must be the genuine article. It had to put the city at a respectable distance but be close enough for comfortable weekend commuting. However, locale was only part of it. Anyone of his generation would know what he wanted. No transplanted bourgeois suburban brick-and-tile villa would do. The spirit of the shack had to be right, its character set preferably somewhere in the 1950s. It would need a properly casual, even run-down, beach air. It should have a verandah to sleep weekend guests, a working septic system, an open fireplace and somewhere to hang a dartboard. A glimpse at least of the Pacific through the trees was mandatory.

In his head David carried a clear picture of weekends in his shack. For a start there would be no television. He and Lydia would surf and make love in the afternoon to Rolling Stones tapes and read best-sellers and play Scrabble. On the verandah he and his children would strengthen bonds with quoits and table-tennis. Under his gum trees friends would drink in their swimming costumes and eat grilled fish caught at dawn.

On a sunny spring day with a high swell running from the ocean straight into Broken Bay he had eventually found the shack he wanted on the central coast at Pearl Beach. It was built of weatherboard and fibro-cement, painted the colour of pale clay, and it settled on the hillside sheltered from the southerly wind and facing north along the beach. Its ceiling contained a possum's nest or two, and three mature gums, and a jacaranda in bloom filtered the gleam off the sea. The Recession was forcing the owners, a writer and her husband, to rapidly consolidate their assests and their price was reasonable. Apologetically they pointed out an old ceiling stain of possum urine. David laughed. He liked their honesty about the possum pee, the view of the surf from the wooden balcony and the lizards warming on the railing, and, in his new mood of independence and self-assertion, made them an offer. The nostalgic boom of waves had punctuated their negotiations.

An anticipatory air had overlain this weekend. David was looking forward to showing the shack to the children. This was also their first meeting with Lydia and he hoped the shack would break the ice. Along the Newcastle Expressway things looked optimistic. They sang along with the radio and Helena chattered happily to Lydia. Just beyond the Gosford exit warm spring whiffs of eucalypt pollen and the fecund muddy combustion of subtropical undergrowth suddenly filled the car with the scents of holidays.

'Not long to summer,' he pronounced.

'That's a funny name,' Helena said, pointing. 'Mooney Mooney Creek.'

'Mooney Mooney loony,' Tim burbled.

The police hadn't caught the killer, or killers, and according to the news were completely mystified. Both victims had been married to other people, but the spouses had been unaware of the affair and were not under suspicion. *Thrill Killing?* the tabloids wondered. The lovers, both in their thirties, had driven all the way from Sydney's western suburbs for their tryst by the creek. Oyster farmers on the Hawkesbury had seen their car burning at 5.00 a.m. Later people remembered hearing the high-pitched revving of an engine and perhaps some human cries.

'I hope there's some good surf,' Paul said. His board was strapped to the roof-rack. As usual lately he was alternately amiable and taciturn, in the sixteen-year-old-fashion, but did not give the impression as he often did that this was a duty weekend.

Lydia was anxious to please and turned back to smile at him, 'I'm sure there will be.'

It was dark when they reached Pearl Beach. For five minutes David fumbled about in the oleander and hibiscus bushes which scraped against the walls, searching for the fuse box where the old owners had left the key. As he stamped around the periphery lighting matches something rustled in a tree above him and a gumnut dropped with a clatter on the tin roof and rolled into the guttering. Possum, he told himself. A mosquito landed noisily on his cheek. From the black shrubbery Helena gave one of the high indignant screams she had affected since her parents separated. Lately she needed soothing and coddling for every slight and injury, real and imaginary. Meanwhile each cry and sulk, no matter how exaggerated, struck him with a hopelessness, produced a hollow despair in him which made him want to simultaneously embrace and shake her and yell, 'I'm sorry my darling, I love you, and my wounds sting too.'

He found the fuse box and the key and opened the front door. Helena burst inside, her sandals clopping on the wooden floor, crying, 'Paul punched me on the arm!'

'Jesus!' Paul said, sidling in with his sleeping bag. 'I just brushed past her. I wouldn't touch her bloody poxy arm.'

'Easy, you two,' their father said.

Lydia struggled in with a carton of groceries. 'Isn't it cute?' she announced.

'Have you seen it already?' Helena asked suspiciously. 'When did you see it?'

Some mosquitoes had followed them inside and soon had Helena whining. Lydia lit a mosquito coil and hunted up a tube of Stop-Itch. The previous owners had left them a bottle of Chablis in the fridge with a note saying 'Welcome to Marsupial Manor!' David uncorked it immediately and they swigged wine from coffee mugs while he unloaded the car and they settled in.

'What a terrific gesture,' Lydia said.

Making his final trip from the car carrying the Scrabble set, Lydia's handbag and Helena's pillow shaped like a rhinocerous, David saw the others' faces pass across the bright uncurtained windows and he stopped on the path, surprised at how earnest they all appeared, even the younger children, how foreign and intense in their tasks. They were all frowning. He could hear their feet thudding on the bare boards. He heard a low murmur from Paul and then Lydia's face over the sink lit up and she gave a laugh. She put a paper bag on her head like a chef's cap. Tim giggled.

David went inside to join them. From the balcony the night sea was as slick and black as grease in the new-moon light, and fruit bats flapped against the stars.

In the middle of the night David awoke and instantly regretted the cute rusticity of the lavatory and its position some ten metres outside in the bushes. A breezy brick cubicle, it had no electricity and a reasonable prospect of spiders in the darkness. He would have to set something up with extension cords. He took a couple of steps out the back door and pissed into the hibiscus. Back in bed, he was unable to sleep again; these nights if he woke up he always had trouble falling back to sleep. Anxieties churned in his mind until exhaustion eventually took over at dawn.

Funny, the more numerous and wilder his wakeful thoughts, the less imaginative his dreams. Since the breakup his dreams had been uniformly mundane — of buying a loaf of Vogel's sandwich bread, catching the 387 bus into town, reading the television guide — sexless, fact-filled visions in which each action or trans-action was conducted with the utmost solemnity and realism. Perhaps, he told himself, they were subliminal exhortations to live a moderate, conservative life. Whatever, they were so boring and accurate in their triviality that he allowed his bladder to wake him.

And then, back in bed, the sleepless turmoil began.

Why hadn't the lovers run away? His heart pounded in sympathy. The killers must have had a weapon to force them out of their car, to make them remove their clothes, to wound or threaten them sufficiently that they didn't try to escape. Perhaps

114

they did try. Were they chased all over the picnic area?

Was she raped? He presumed so but the papers didn't say. Did their bodies have bullet holes? No idea. Were the bodies too flattened and battered to tell? Considering these horrors, David rolled over on the doughy mattress, his hip bumping against Lydia's warm bottom with a sudden heat and pressure that surprised them both. She murmured in her sleep and turned over.

Their clothes had been found lying unburned a distance from the gutted car, so they'd been dressed when first harassed, not nakedly fornicating such as to inflame the crazy passions of murdering yokels. The killers were likely from these parts. Maybe he had stood alongside them tonight in the hotel bottle shop buying his Dimple Haig. Sandy-haired yobbos with a big gas guzzler throbbing in the car park. He had visions of headlights bearing down on Lydia and him, of them being mesmerised like possums struck by the beam of a torch.

Thump, brake and reverse, wheels spinning crazily in the gravel. Skin and hair on the bumpers.

He told himself the shack was meant to be an antidote to all this.

Amazingly on cue, screams, grunts and thuddings, eerie gurgles and whispers erupted just outside the bedroom window. His scalp prickled, Lydia sat up in terror.

'Just a possum fight,' he calmed her, his chest pounding. He got out of bed again and made them cups of warm milk. Like children they whispered in the foreign room. Her upper lip corners wore a small milky moustache. Stroking each other with an urgent solicitude, they made love aware of daily jeopardy and thin walls.

Father and daughter rose first and early on Saturday morning, murmuring and tiptoeing conspiratorially and taking their orange juice out onto the balcony. A flock of parrots exploded from one of their gum trees. The sun rising out of the Pacific slanted obliquely over their domain and brought a new arrangement of parallel shimmers to the surface of the water below. Instantly David saw he had made one mistake — there was no surf and there would rarely be. Freak conditions had no doubt prevailed the day he inspected the shack, a strange pure easterly perhaps instead of the usual southerly or nor'easter or even westerly. Why hadn't it occurred to him that Box Head would block the nor'easters, Lion Island the southerlies? It didn't matter that their beach faced the open Pacific; there would be no surfing; they would have to drive several kilometres north to swim in the surf. His personal stretch of sea was quiescent, bland as bathwater, nice for fishing, sailboarding and swimming up and down. He felt vaguely sick.

As a boy his happiness had been bound up in the ocean, the regular rising and curling of waves over sandbanks and reefs, the baking sun, the cronies lounging against the promenade, the bunches of girls gossiping and flirting on the sand, the violent contrasting physical pleasures of bodysurfing. In his twenties and early thirties he had still never tired of watching the surf. Like flames it had the capacity to induce a calming trance. It held in store everything from a happy domestic weekend, healthy dawn exercise, to a snappy hangover cure. But over the past few years, through work and travel and the particular, strangely inevitable manner in which his marriage had frayed, then unravelled, he'd lost the habit of those peculiarly satiating Australian days.

He'd liked sharing them and Angela had lost interest; or perhaps among their other discarded mutual interests they had just forgotten them.

Lydia was a bodysurfer.

Lydia had become a keen bodysurfer since knowing him. She had a history as an initiator of extreme physical incidents, as an experimenter and a changer of circumstances. She had already tried abseiling, hang-gliding, show-jumping, scuba-diving and their sexual counterparts. From his watchful position ten years further along the track he could detect in her a vulnerability to danger and a risky wilfulness with the potential to carry her, and others, over the edge. But they matched each other perfectly, blended harmoniously, gripped and floated. In the surf her recklessness made him laugh, the way she launched herself into definite dumpers, surfacing shakily in the foam with a breast out of her bathers, her hair in her eyes and a fist raised in mock victory.

Sitting yawning with his ten-year-old daughter in the quiet early sunlight he tried to pin down the exact sensation of those old ocean days. It was a combination of the exhilarating charge of the surf, the plunge on a wave, the currents pummelling and streaming along the body, the skin stretched salty and taut across the shoulders, the pungent sweetness of suntan oil, the sensual anticipation of future summer days and nights. Certainly he had never been as happy since. Therefore he could hardly be blamed for trying for that feeling again — the harmony and boundless optimism. And he had got it only half right.

Helena snuggled up to him in their warm patch in the treetops. Birds squabbled around them but they seemed the only humans awake anywhere. The world of sea and bush was comatose. He thought of Lydia buried in the valley of the saggy double bed; Paul in his sleeping bag, mouth open, hair awry; Tim flushed and cupid-lipped on the night-and-day. And Angela in her shared Mosman bed under the Amish hand-sewn quilt he had bought her in Pennsylvania. In white stitching the old Amish lady had signed her quilt 'Mrs B. Yoder'. They didn't believe in cosmetics, cars or radios but Mrs Yoder took American Express. He did not want Helena and Timmy snuggling under the quilt for early morning cuddles with the occupants. He did not want the quilt *involved*.

Kissing the crown of Helena's head, he inhaled her parting.

'Want a swim before breakfast, my sweet?' he asked.

She was delighted. 'A secret swim,' he told her. Somehow he wanted to bind her in a conspiracy. He wanted to serve her up private soothing information about their present and future. Holding hands they padded barefoot down the road to the beach. Cool clay squashed under their toes as the sun began to slant over their path. Crows and currawongs fluttered clumsily in the bushes. Under the cliff face the sea baths were like glass. Helena was the bolder. Without hesitating she ran to the deep end and dived in. The coldness shocked him when he joined her; he had to swim three lengths of the pool before his circulation adjusted to the temperature. His daughter's body gave no hint of the cold. She had been having swimming coaching and he was surprised at her new neat prowess, the precise arm strokes slicing into the pool, the efficient three-stroke breathing. When they climbed out she flicked water at him, giggling coquettishly, wiggling her chubby backside and smoothing back her wet hair in parody of a hundred women in shampoo commercials. He noticed her breasts were just starting to grow and she flapped her hands over them while she jigged about. It jolted him that she would cease being a child. It was only the other day she'd been born, a month overdue, in the end chemically induced. She hadn't wanted to join the world then. If only he could warn her, 'Stop now while there's still time. You don't want to get into this can of worms.'

As they left the beach he was still phrasing what he wanted to say to her, at the same time hoping that his message was somehow being telepathically understood, absorbed through the pores.

Finally he said, 'I love you, my sweet,' brushing sand from his feet.

'Me too,' she said. 'Daddy, can I play the Space Invaders?'

At the beach store she played a video game while he bought

milk and the papers. The picnic ground murders were still page one of the local paper. Tests were proceeding on the woman's body to determine whether she had been 'assaulted' prior to her death. The extent of the 'injuries' made this difficult. Police asked citizens to immediately report any vehicle with suspicious dents or bloodstains.

Hand in hand they walked back to the shack. 'Can I have my ears pierced, Daddy?' she asked.

'Perhaps when you're older. It doesn't look nice on little girls.'

She was still whining as they walked inside. 'I don't want to hear any more about it,' he said.

Their mid-morning procession to the beach gave the impression of a cartoon jungle safari. Balancing his surfboard on his head, Paul amiably led the single file, followed by a talkative Helena with her flippers and swimming goggles, Lydia carrying her big bag of beach paraphernalia — towels, suntan cream, insect repellent, baby oil and magazines; Tim, the youngest, travelling light and scot-free as usual, dragging a stick in the clay, and David, bringing the Esky of sandwiches and drinks. They had decided on a picnic lunch. 'Bonga, bonga,' boomed the father, imitating native drums. 'Bonga, bonga,' repeated Helena and Tim all the way down to the sand.

Now the beach was warm, and in its most populated section near the baths, relatively noisy. Children splashed in the baths and shrieked in the shallows. Small wavelets plopped on the shore. Paul had already observed from the balcony the sorry state of the waves but had perversely brought his board anyway, as if to indicate to this soft elderly crowd that this was by no means his element. They dropped their things on the sand and the younger children raced into the water. With a superior grin at the sea Paul flopped down in the sand. 'Top waves, Dad.'

'Give us a break,' his father said, collapsing too.

Next to him Lydia was arranging her towel on a level patch of sand, ironing away lumps and wrinkles and placing her beach appurtenances within reach. Then she removed her bikini top and, her breasts quivering, the nipples wide and brown in the sun, she sat down. Reaching for the suntan cream from her bag, she rubbed some briskly into her breasts with a studious circular motion, paying attention to the nipples. More cream was squeezed onto the stomach and legs, even the tops of the feet.

David was slightly unnerved, as usual, by the act of public revelation (there always seemed to be some sort of statement underlying their sudden exposure among other people), but he had never realised how much her naked breasts actually *moved*. They had three definite motions — they were simultaneously bouncing, swinging and shivering. From the prim, diligent way she pursed her lips while she applied the cream she seemed to be either terribly solicitous of them or disapproving of their independent lives.

David avoided looking at them too openly. Ogling was out of the question. He did, however, glance surreptitiously at his elder son, but Paul, though hardly able to miss them, was staring coolly seawards.

Completing this display, still with a frown of concentration, Lydia flicked a grain of sand from one glistening aureole, spread more cream deftly over her face, and then lay back on her towel with a sigh of contentment. 'I wonder what the poor people are doing,' she said.

I wonder if women know what they're doing, David wondered. How did those tits which had been used to sexually tempt him at 3.00 a.m. suddenly at 11.30 become as neutral as elbows? Who's kidding who? He was too far gone at thirty-eight, especially after the past couple of years, to read the fine print any more, much less try to keep up with the constant changes in the rules. They were amazing, leave it at that. He was awestruck by the grey areas, the skating-over, the 180-degree turns that women made these days. The breakup and his new status, or lack of status, had made him hypersensitive to the female dichotomies — fashion versus politics, the desperate clash between ideals and glands — and their magical sleight of hand which not only hid it all and kept the audience clapping but left you with a coin up your nose or an egg in your ear.

Lying back under the sun he had to smile at the way Lydia pretended she had no exhibitionist's flair, that she didn't love to flaunt what she had, come on strong. He remembered the actual broad-daylight fuck precipitated by those exposed breasts not long ago on Scarborough Beach down south during their search for the perfect shack. They were sunbaking like this after a surf. A nipple brushed his arm accidentally, then insistently. Then began a sly stroking of his thigh, feathery touches over his groin. The sun, the ocean, the whole salty, teasing, teenage delight of it all! They'd got up without a word and strolled determinedly to the end of the beach and, behind a low cairn of rocks barely higher than their horizontal bodies, momentarily hidden from at least fifty beach fishermen, surfers and swimmers, had a most satisfying quickie in the sand.

Their single-mindedness had surprised and amused him later. 'I thought that might work,' she'd said, grinning as they sauntered back to their belongings. 'Was that like your adolescent days? I must say you were very neat — not a drop of sand in me.'

Tim and Helena ran up from the shore, sandy and squabbling.

'He's using bottom words again,' Helena complained. 'He's saying poo and bum and vagina all the time and he keeps throwing sand.'

'I didn't say vagina, I said Virginia.'

'You said vagina!' Abruptly she began to cry, turning away from them and sobbing despairingly.

'I didn't,' Tim screamed. 'You're a liar!' Overcome with rage and emotion, he fell on the sand and kicked and threshed, his yells turning to shrill cries as he kicked sand in his eyes.

'My God!' shouted David, jumping to his feet. 'What's got into you both? Do you want a hiding?'

'Shee-it,' Paul said. 'He does that all the time lately. What that kid needs is some discipline. Come here, stupid, and I'll get the sand out.'

Lydia had her arms round Helena. 'No one will play with us, Helena sobbed. 'It's boring here.'

Lydia said, 'I feel like a swim. Let's go.'

The father sank back on the sand. Leaning back on his elbows, breathing deeply, he watched the trio race each other down to the water, Tim stopping sharply at the edge, hanging back and then wading in gingerly, the others plunging in recklessly. Lydia and Helena surfaced and pushed back their hair and jumped and splashed like any ten-year-olds. They shared unselfconsciousness; if anything Lydia seemed the wilder and giddier, standing on her hands, somersaulting and gambolling, and all the time her breasts swung and fluttered in the sun and water.

Tim was beginning to grizzle at being excluded. Sighing loudly, Paul sauntered down to him, hoisted him up in his arms and strode into the water, joining the splashing females. Paul tossed his little brother around like a beach-ball while Tim shrieked with excitement.

Squinting against the glare, David was relieved and gladdened to see his children and Lydia frolicking together in the sea. It wasn't a familiar scene from his marriage, more like one from his own early childhood, a link to it, a summer holiday at the seaside, a rare time when adults dropped their guard and pretensions and acted the goat. He was aware of the sting of the sun on his neck and this too made him happy; the clean buff-coloured sand, the fringe of gum trees, the dusty blue labiate hills, the turquoise vista of the Pacific all uplifted him. Buoyant, he looked over his shoulder and through the jacaranda picked out the balcony of the shack where his and Helena's red and blue towels were drying on the railing. A warm haze gave the shack's roof an uncertain wavy outline, and parrots still screeched in his trees.

Oddly drawn to this setting, attracted to it but, perhaps because of its newness, detached from it, he half-expected to see his children, Lydia, even himself, stroll out on to the balcony and wave a jaunty towel. But they were playing in the sea. He was lounging on the sand. Paul was lifting Tim on his shoulders. Paul's tanned back and shoulder muscles were suddenly sharply defined by the weight, and patterns of sinews moved in his arms and shoulders. Among the shrill giggles his deeper laughter rang out. Lydia was similarly hoisting Helena on to her shoulders — with difficulty — and the action threw back her shoulders and pushed out her chest and almost collapsed her in splashes and giggles.

David watched the couples face each other — grinning, dripping knights on horseback — and heard the yells of encouragement, the snorts and laughter, and saw the infection of excitability strike them. He sat in the sun with a cold constriction in his throat as the riders wrestled and the horses alternately collided and retreated, striking and sliding against each other in the shallows, softness against muscle.

If David could have spoken satisfactorily to Lydia next morning he might have described his dream that night thus:

It began with me driving an Avis car fast and north through scrubby country on a hot, dry day. The highway was clear, the airconditioning cool, and on the radio old favourites kept my fingers tapping on the wheel. Bugs smeared themselves on the windscreen, but I obliterated them with automatic spray and wipers, the wipers stroking as elegantly as conductors' batons. The car's tyres made a satisfying drumming sound on the tarred joins in the highway paving, a repetitive noise of power and resolve. All this registered on me strongly — the sense of purpose was heightened because the car had been freshly cleaned and the hygienic vinyl scent of the upholstery was high in my head.

I drove for a time, for what seemed like an hour, and from the changing vegetation — the trees were becoming even more stunted and sparse, the wild oats and veldt grass fringing the highway ever dryer and barely covering the sandy ground — I gathered that I was nearing the coast. An arrowed sign said *Aurora — 10 km* and I followed it, turning left off the highway.

A wind sprang up as the car left the protection of the hills and it whipped sand drifts across the road. The road cut through sand dunes spread patchily with pigface and tumbleweeds and led obliquely to the sea — every now and then I saw a slice of blue between the white dunes before it disappeared again. Another, bigger sign said *Aurora — 5 km* below a logotype of a leaping dolphin against the sun, and I followed it, the car planing occasionally through the sand drifts.

Soon I came to an indication of habitation: a gold dome-shaped building, a sort of civic centre, flying a flag carrying the dolphin-and-sun logo. Before its entrance was a statue carved out of limestone, apparently of King Neptune. Surrounding the gold dome was a flat grassy field, which was kept green and free of the sand drifts, I presumed, from the parallel lines of sprinklers and the presence of five or six heavy rollers, only with great municipal perseverance. As I pulled up two children came over one of the adjacent dunes and slid down it on sleds until they came to rest on the grass. I called out to them, wanting to ask further directions, but they grabbed up their sleds and climbed back up the dune as fast as they could struggle in the sand. I tried the gold building next. From a sharp cloudless sky the sun struck its gleaming surface with such a dazzling glare it was impossible to approach it without squinting. Anyway, the front doors were closed — presumably it was some sort of public holiday here — and the only other sign of life was a nervously hissing bobtail goanna which displayed its blue tongue at me from a clump of pigface by the entrance. A thin pungent smell of decaying seaweed was carried to me on the breeze.

The road circled the gold building and continued, so I drove on, still travelling slantingly towards the ocean, and around the next sandhill I saw the first rotary clothes hoist sticking up in the dunes like a lone palm in the desert, and then more of them, some skeletal, others blooming with washing, and, behind them, facing the sea, a scattering of suburban houses straight from the middle-class outskirts of any western city in the world. In this moonscape the range of architectural styles was unusually extreme, even impressive, in its randomness and unfittingness to the arid environment and climate: mock-Tudor nestled hard up against Mediterranean villa, then came three or four bleak, windswept blocks dotted with FOR SALE signs, a Cape Cod or two, some ranch-modern experiments and an Australian-Romanesque edifice. They did, however, have some features in common: two shiny cars and a cabin cruiser on a trailer sat in every driveway. A sprinkler whirred in each front garden; there were no fences but walls had been cleverly erected to shield the grass and the cars from the sea breeze. The backyards had no shelter and, while the sprinklers whirred in the front, the clothes hoists, with a steady grating hum, spun like catherine wheels in the wind. It was easy to see which way it blew — the clothes hoists all leaned like cypresses from the sou' westerly.

Suddenly the sledding children returned: they were Max and

Paul. This was no surprise, the appearance together of my brother and my son, both now the same age — about eight or nine — and similarly skinny, brown-skinned and with their freckled and peeling noses and cheeks coated in zinc cream.

'In there, you nong,' Max said, pointing out a pink-brick home with a 1950s skillion roof. Max was right in that it *was* my mother who came to the door in a Liberty print brunch coat over a swimming costume, gave me an amiable kiss on the cheek and led me inside.

I know I must have seemed exasperated. 'God, I've been searching for ages,' I complained. I was actually immensely relieved. Relief flooded over me and intervening time was abruptly concertinaed into days, hours. 'You made it a bit difficult.'

My mother smiled, a little embarrassed, holding her mouth in a constrained way, like the time she had her teeth capped. 'I know, Davey. It took me a while to make adjustments.' There seemed some strain to the left side of her face, a tautness in the skin that she was shy about. Otherwise she looked very well, and I said so.

'Getting there,' she smiled. 'The dolphins keep me young.'

'They would,' I agreed. 'What do you hear from Dad?'

'Ask him yourself,' she said. 'Let's go down to the boatel.'

We drove off down the road, Amphitrite Avenue, I noticed, with me asking inane questions about her new Volvo — was she happy with the safety features, et cetera? — and presently she indicated another limestone statue of King Neptune, with trident, this one about thirty feet high, rising out of the dunes.

'I like it,' she declared firmly. 'Rex thinks it's vulgar, but I like it. The boatel's near here, in Poseidon Place.'

Was this a delicate situation? Separate living quarters? I kept my questions to myself, however, as we drew up to the Triton Boatel, a dun-coloured limestone structure built right on the edge of the ocean like a Moorish fort. Radiating out from it was a long limestone breakwater sheltering hundreds of pleasure craft, their stays and moorings rattling and tinkling in the wind — yachts, launches and power boats of all sizes and varieties, even a Chinese junk — though their owners, or any people at all, were not to be seen.

We sauntered along a sort of fake gangplank into the boatel lobby, Mum tripping very brightly through the foyer, I thought. She had discarded her brunch coat and looked very tanned and fit in her green Lastex swimsuit, just like the old Jantzen girl trademark.

Dad was behind the counter in his neat summer seersucker. He waved off my enthusiastic greeting, smiling apologetically. 'It's the off-season,' he said. 'We're still settling in, David. The last chap ran the place down. An Iraqi or something.'

'It's very presentable,' I told him. He looked a bit fidgety, though happy enough.

'The boatel business has got to expand,' he asserted stoutly. 'I couldn't wait to get here, I can tell you. Best decision I ever made, running my own show.'

'It's certainly an interesting proposition, Dad.' For some reason he was a little skittish in my company.

'All units right on the ocean, waterbeds in every room, colour TV, fully equipped kitchen, mid-week linen change where applicable. It's got to go like a bomb.'

We left Dad adjusting his Diners Club brochures in their little display stand. My mother was anxious to show me over the marine park. 'Don't worry about him,' she said. 'He's really as keen as I am about the whole Aurora concept.'

It was surprisingly not beyond my comprehension to learn that my mother was leading a new life as a vivacious dolphin communicator. She certainly looked the part as she proudly swept me in to the Aurora Marine Park, the sun catching the blonde streaks in

127

her hair and highlighting her brown, slender limbs. She tossed a silver whistle briskly from hand to hand.

'Activity. Activity-plus is the message humming through Aurora,' she said.

What was new to me was my parents' sudden boundless punchy optimism. I felt slack and middle-aged by comparison; pale, short of wind.

Mum knifed into the pool then, and surfaced balanced on the backs of two dolphins, smiling fit for television. Her charges were just as energetic, jumping and squeaking and snorting through those holes in their heads. She had names for them, unapt modern children's names like Jasmine and Trent and Jason and Bree, and conducted some sort of affectionate dialogue using her whistle while they squirmed self-congratulatingly out of the water and bumped up a ramp towards us like sleek blow-up toys, their grey tongues waggling disgustingly at her.

'Do you speak dolphin, David?' she asked me out of the side of her mouth.

'No, I never learned.'

'I'm particularly fascinated in people exploring the intricacies of the dolphin language,' she went on. 'It's taught in the school here, you know.' She gestured vaguely. 'Humans learn it too.' And then she began speaking warmly to Bree, Trent and company in fractured schoolgirl French. They replied similarly, their beaks actually quite well formed for the nasalities and their accents rather better than my mother's. Fishy vowels hung in the air.

'Think you could hack it here?' Mum asked me suddenly, an arm each around Jason and Trent. 'Je t'aime,' she murmured to Jason, unnecessarily I thought, raking her inch-long red nails down his tongue. He crooned appreciatively.

'I don't know,' I said. Her jargon jolted, also her recently acquired fondness for animals. She didn't even allow us to have a dog.

128

'You could be an aquarist,' she suggested, 'helping Damian with the makos and hammerheads.'

'What about Dad at the boatel?'

'If you prefer.' *Allez!* she exclaimed suddenly and blew a blast on her whistle. The dolphins bounced back into the pool. 'You know something?' my mother said to me conversationally, and the sunlight on the sheen of her swimsuit was so glaring it hurt my eyes, 'It may be perpetual summer here but I'm against adultery.'

'Who isn't, Mum?' I said.

'So put that in your pipe and smoke it,' she said.

In the Sunday papers there was nothing about the picnic ground murders. David thought it looked as if the police had put the case in their too-hard basket. He spent most of the day reading alone while the others swam or played Scrabble or, in the children's case, the video games at the store. Mid-afternoon he got them packed up and moving early, he said, to avoid the traffic back to the city. Driving fast to get home, and in deep thought, he crossed Mooney Mooney Creek without noticing.

Eighty Per Cent Humidity

On Paul Lang's worst day since being extruded from the employment market he makes several bad discoveries. In ascending order of disruption and confusion rather than chronologically they are the flat battery in his old Toyota, the lump on his penis and the lesbian love poem in his girlfriend's handbag.

The last mentioned discovery, on top of the heat and the eighty per cent humidity and his grinding hangover, drives him in ever decreasing circles from room to room evading the sunlight and finally past Faye, still lounging in bed checking her stars in the *Sunday Telegraph*, and out of the flat into the street without a word.

The morning sun sliding through the chinks in the bamboo blinds had given her body a sly tiger skin effect. Only the sides of his eyes could look at her and slip away. Too breathless to speak, he stuck the poem on the fridge door behind a magnetised plastic pineapple and left. More than left, vanished. Vaporised.

This is where he retreats into his core, stamps down the stairs scattering cats and tries to start his car, take off, drive far from Bondi, and discovers the flat battery. Not a kick. Paul could get hysterical at this stage weren't it for the pressure booming in his ears and a sensation of increasing concavity at the temples. Slamming the car door he moves heavily towards the security of Mario's thick aromas.

Humidity is enhancing the smells, sending their tendrils out to jolt the senses of passers-by. The usual wild-eyed locals are at large: junked-up rhythm guitarists and New Zealand maintenance dodgers not yet down from Saturday night, munching fast fried foods and planning survival routines. Cackling juvenile surfers sit on the kerb picking their toes. Against an ocean backdrop the first Japanese of the day photograph each other uncertainly. A blondish woman with a fixed religious smile verges up to Paul and presses a pamphlet on him. He accepts it absent-mindedly, meanders around everyone, smoking a cigarette with discomfort.

Mario's bins are festering out the front, last night's prawn cocktail and snapper mornay remnants stewing in the heat. Holding his breath, Paul slides through the door into the café, down the back into the gloom with his darker fancies, and sits down at a table as new waves of surprise and fury arrive and revolve.

When they met up at Byron Bay in his surfing days she said she had never been in love — but she had been 'in lust'. This announcement was boldly but self-consciously delivered in front of him and her then boyfriend, Andrew of the serene brown eyes. She had been an enthusiast of 'pure, unadulterated fun' in unusual quarters, she hinted over some local dope and Hunza pie, but later recanted. After she went off with him she said such past affairs were only to be expected of this era and other circumstances. To his questions both tentative and explicit she effortlessly gave the wrong answers. He took it she was in love with him because she said so, but what would she know? Her life story was full of modest lies and wide omissions. She had the slyness and eye wrinkles of an extra ten years. She censored scenes of bliss. Women are patient and men are not.

There is an explosion as Mario's orange juice squeezing machine starts up like a Boeing, grates and roars. It sounds as if it is chewing and mangling the oranges, skins and all.

He should have seen it in her intensity and steady black eyes. The first time he saw her her body seemed to quiver under the skin. At the sight of her the afternoon turned to madness. He was in the Byron Bay newsagent's buying torch batteries for camping. There was a hand on his arm and a blissed-out bearded type said, 'Save your money, man. I've got a hint that'll save you on lighting. Electricity, batteries, even candles.'

'Oh, really.' Then he saw this typical thirty-five-year-old sixties hangover was accompanied by a black-eyed woman with a level gaze. She was about thirty, slim and tanned and naked under her caftan. She drew his eyes while this perfect stranger rabbited on about energy economy. They were Andrew and Faye, local residents and alternative culture couple. It turned out that Andrew was beating back the Recession with tampons and margarine.

'They give you a more romantic light and a nicer dispersal,' Andrew announced loudly in the shop. 'We use them all the time, Faye and I.'

And she winked.

'They burn for ever and you get some great effects. I cover them with a coloured shade. It disperses the light really beautifully. I'm into imaginative light dispersal.'

On the footpath they offered him a joint and, shuffling in his thongs, he received her signals, every one, and couldn't leave.

'Any old oil,' Andrew instructed. 'Meadow Lea margarine, safflower oil is fine. Pour it in an ashtray, a soy sauce dish, what-have-you. Get a tampon, put one end in the oil, hang the other over the edge of the saucer. It sucks up the oil, you know. Take it easy, though. Too far in and you've drowned it, too moist and you've got a bit of smoke and flame. Light the string as a wick. Bingo!'

Andrew demonstrated one of his tampon lamps over dinner.

Flames leapt a foot, smoke filled the galvanised iron room. 'You like a lower flame, use only a thin strand of the tampon,' Andrew recommended. It was hard to imagine Andrew as a science student back at Geelong Grammar. It was hard to imagine Faye with him for long and she wasn't three days later.

Driving south in the Toyota, she said, 'You know why I love you?'

'I couldn't guess,' Paul said.

'Because you can come five times on a milkshake and a muesli bar.'

He must have appeared shocked. 'That was a joke,' she said.

Mario's could rise from its foundations with the din of the juice machine. The poem mentioned the works, nothing euphemistic, enough lyrical and romantic personal obscenities for him to mull over for the next thirty or forty years, plenty to give him the shivers now, literally set him shaking in his seat as Yvonne, the diminutive Maori waitress, materialises alongside smelling musky.

Paul needs protein, Vitamin C, carbohydrates to recover and live. He checks the twenty dollar note in his pocket. That's it until dole day. 'Juice!' he tries to shout over the clatter of the machine. 'Toasted cheese sandwich! Cappuccino!' Yvonne smiles anxiously, lowering her lip over a diagonally snapped tooth, a present from Albert, her Samoan boyfriend, on Christmas Eve, and bends low, putting an ear to Paul's mouth.

'Come again,' she says. He breathes his order into her black hair, his nose nudging her earrings. Yvonne wears two together halfway up one ear and they look odd though satisfactory, he thinks, a nice exotic touch. The little musk-smelling ear looks sympathetic enough to nuzzle. Faye has no lobes, which presents earring problems, but not, he imagines, if she had her ears pierced like Yvonne's.

He's becoming irrational. He notices he is unwrapping sugar

cubes and building a little igloo on the table.

The juice machine judders to a halt but Mario, a believer that silence indicates a lack of proper capitalist intentions, substitutes for its uproar a tape of 'House of the Rising Sun'. Its volume and sentiments go badly against Paul's grain. Outside the café tourist buses are pulling up, discharging loads of denimed Japanese honeymooners, but the exterior smell and interior ambience of Mario's do not tempt them to enter. Lighting another cigarette with many a twitch, Paul suddenly remembers his lump, swept away by more dramatic events.

An accurate prod is not possible here; neither, for that matter, was a full inspection carried out on discovery in the headachy dawn. His hungover head had driven him first to her handbag for her period-pain Myadols, thus to her hymn to lip, nipple and vulva. Belonging to one Joanne. Blank verse with a fascinated stress on the softness of textures. Touches, kisses, jokes and giggles. Again in anguish he forgets his lump. *Joanne?*

He is in a trance. Surprised, he sees the blonde woman's pamphlet on the table, a screed in the form of a comic strip for slow wits featuring a character called Sam the Super Surfer. At his present ebb Paul sucks a sugar cube and reads:

Sam was given his first surfboard at the age of ten.

From then on it was down to the beach and surf, surf, surf.

Before long Sam was real good, by far the best surfer on the beach.

He started entering local comps. And winning.

Pretty soon he had become national champ. Before too long he was taking out big prizes on the international circuit.

Hawaii, California. Life at the top for Sam was pretty cruisy.

He became world champ and rode the crest of a huge wave of popularity.

136

Sam had everything he always wanted. Money, cars and plenty of girls, girls, girls.

He didn't have to work any more for a living. Or even wax his surfboard. He paid someone else to do it.

But Sam was enjoying himself so much that he neglected the most important thing — practice.

One day the bubble burst. Along came Hotfoot Harry and took the world title.

Sam was stunned. He was all washed up and his lifelong dream was over.

As he turned to go someone put his hand on his shoulder. It was Ken the Contest Organiser.

'You know, Sam,' said Ken kindly. 'We all have bad breaks sometimes. But there's someone we can lean on when life gets us down. His name is Jesus.'

'By receiving Christ's life into us we are "born again" and become children of God.'

'Jesus said, "Unless a man is born again he cannot enter the Kingdom of God." You must be born again.'

'John 3, verses 3 to 5,' added Ken with a smile.

Sam thought about what Ken had said. Then he replied, 'I'd like to give my life to Jesus, but how do I do it?'

'Easy,' Ken replied. 'Just kneel on the sand and pray after me right now.'

So Sam gave his life to Jesus. And he discovered that while being a Super Surfer was great, it was not as great as knowing Jesus.

No matter what sort of a surfer you are, you can ask Jesus into your life.

Don't wipe out when you can be stoked on Jesus.

Paul has a clear image of Ken the Contest Organiser. Ken is a boy-scoutish thirty-five-year-old, square-jawed, tanned, with a clipboard and a natty Piz Buin eyeshade, and a matey slap on the buttocks. Ken encourages cold showers, communal and boisterous. Ken turns up at the after-contest dance without a girl once again and suggests a Big Mac and a lift home in his car and, gosh, what a terrific view of the surf tonight, doesn't it stoke you, might stop for just a minute, Jesus or no Jesus.

Men are not close to God, even if there is one, thinks Paul. Women are nearer. From old Catholic ladies to your average nymphomaniac, he's never met one who was honestly an unbeliever. He used to believe females were just generally nicer, remembering birthdays, keeping busy and scrupulously hiding farts. Women were better people. Until this recent revelation. And now he knows why they're such Christians: the hypocrisy appeals to them.

Yvonne approaches with his food and sets it down in a gentle fashion. Her T-shirt displays the diameter of her nipples. The business with the lip over the tooth makes her seem shyer than she used to be and he likes the change. She potters around the table, adjusting cutlery and tentatively creating a presence.

'Where's Faye?'

He shrugs and makes a slicing motion with his hand, a horizontal karate chop of resignation and finality. The air motion blows Sam the Super Surfer to the floor. Yvonne bends and picks up the pamphlet and gives it a quizzical glance.

'Heavy,' she remarks. Then she announces, 'Albert's going Orange.'

'Rajneesh?'

'Right. Another bouncer at Abe's put him onto it. The Rastafarian thing never sat easily — his hair wouldn't work. He says he's tired of everyday violence. He sees the world in a new serene light through Bhagwan.'

138

'Is it the clothes or the serenity? I didn't take Albert for mystical.'

She fingers the tooth. 'With the other thing, as far as he could ascertain Haile Selassie never made it to Samoa. This one's a challenge, getting the colours right. But they're not so stuck on orange these days. Pinks, reds, maroons, there's quite a range. I saw a Rajneesh guy up the Cross the other night in a red Pierre Cardin suit, very stylish. I don't mind all that. You seen the bumper stickers? "Jesus Saves, Moses Invests, Bhagwan Spends."'

'Albert doesn't need the encouragement.'

'Another thing, they teach you you can fuck anyone.'

Paul's right eye gives a twitch. 'Compulsory, is it, like the colour scheme?'

Yvonne grabs up his cigarette from the ashtray and draws on it savagely. 'Some Orange chick gives him a dose and he's out on his Samoan arse.'

As she flicks away an old Hungarian regular is looking up from his coffee and staring at her breasts with a pale intensity. His cheeks are almost translucent; the blue veins show through the skin. Yvonne is still in a state. 'Can I get you anything?' she demands, shaking them deliberately.

'No zenk you.'

'Not even a pig knuckle?' she calls over her shoulder as she skims through the kitchen doors.

Breakfast is stretching to its limit but Paul is loath to leave the security of Mario's. He prolongs his coffee into tortured pornographic imaginings, grainy sauna scenes, bath and bedroom epics featuring the newly compliant Faye and a representative range of performers: brunette spectacled businesswoman types (who let their hair down dramatically), spunky freckled beach girls, a leathered German prison camp wardress or two. Women will take bossiness from other women. Men are dopey innocents, trusting and bumpy as old Labradors. Women are smooth, create secrets and carouse like cobwebs against each other. Did the taste of Joanne come into her mouth as she trimmed and tailored her background material for him? Paul begins to secretly cry.

He must be in a bad way for his thoughts to now turn sentimentally homeward — to beach, school, teenage raging and roast dinners. Abruptly he suffers remorse. Lately he hasn't been a wonderboy son. He has flown in the face of their proud expectations. Kind, contemporary Mum and Dad had allowed him to sample the Californian education system and Malibu and Huntington Beach with its oil derricks on the bloody sand and La Jolla Cove, not to mention Disneyland and Alcatraz. Who else did he know who had discussed his future as an intelligent and creative adult in a funky restaurant in Santa Barbara often frequented by the Ronald Reagans? They weren't there that day.

('What do you think you'd like to do, Paul?'

'I've boiled it down to either painting or film directing.'

'Terrific,' enthused creative Dad, looking up the latest David Hockney exhibition and booking on the Universal Studios tour. Dad liked what Hockney did with Los Angeles swimming pools: 'Amazing for an Englishman, he gets the water just right.' A minor sorrow of Dad's life was that Hockney was (a) homosexual, and (b) an artistic interpreter of still water rather than surf. Dad suggested that when Paul was a famous painter too he could rectify this, fill the art vacuum for heterosexual, surf-obsessed sensualists.)

This was one family with never a squabble on the generation-gap classics — hair and clothing, drugs, drink and driving; rational discussion instead on politics and the drug problem over a Sunday morning backyard beer. And attention had been paid to his own thin-skinned feelings all the way up to, during and after the split. Only he hadn't realised the split was going on! What a shock! He'd still been getting reconciled to the idea of them fucking *each other* much less other people.

Some mornings he woke, and for a second he was still a kid and they were all together and everything was sunny and comfortable. There was a particular light coming through the window that recalled holidays, and the future's farthest reaches were six weeks away.

Paul can't adjust to the existence of sex this morning. He dries his eyes feeling cynical, bruised and self-righteous. He hasn't the mental or physical energy to sort out the battery problem just yet. Perhaps a swim will help straighten him out.

As he farewells Yvonne and crosses the street from the café the beach is already dotted with sunbathers and a heavy surf is breaking over a shallow bank near the shore. Narcissists are on display. Bare breasts flash, fleshy buttocks devour their G-strings, oiled couples slither and smoodge. Unhappily, Paul scuffs along, finds a bare section of territory next to three off-duty Hari Krishnas and stretches out.

While the Faye question throbs in the foreground it is hard to redirect his present, much less his neglected future. The problem of somewhere to live suddenly arises. Still in the flat are his clothes and books, his tri-fin and his painting materials. The money difficulty looms larger than ever. And overlaying everything is the general problem of what his father would call 'attitude and character'.

The trouble is, as he often told Faye, he likes to control his own destiny, hates to feel plucked up and swept along by the fates. (He was no fan of her tarots, astrology and palm-reading.) The fates unfortunately include organised learning and relations with the commercial community. His three retrenchments proved him right. After the last he chose to withhold his presence from further such activities. In his private moments Paul yearns for effortless fame.

In this mood he considers going home to Mosman, but quickly discards it. His mother has a 'friend' called Gordon. ('Dear, I'd like you to meet my friend, Gordon.') *Friend!* Come off it, Mum. Until today the shock of his life had been seeing the empty champagne bottle on her bedside table. Two glasses. He'd just been looking for clean socks. He can't go home.

His father? His father's patience finally ran out in the lounge bar of the Lord Dudley. Before a crackling fire, in a tasteful atmosphere of middle-class desperates chatting up girls with Rugby anecdotes and business wisecracks, they drank Guinness while Dad wrote out a cheque.

'I'm afraid this is the last,' he said. 'You're twenty and you don't stick at things.'

It was peculiar that when people screwed up their lives they wanted everyone around them to act with greater wisdom and responsibility.

Paul was so mortified he could have bolted. His father was rehearsed. His hand was shaking as he wrote the cheque. His voice was very quiet and hurt and his face had a wistful, ageing smile, an and-I-was-pinning-all-my-hopes-on-you-son smile.

'You want to be a painter who doesn't paint,' his father said. 'Before that you were a student who didn't study, who became a surfer who didn't surf. All this aggressive laziness is a pretty shitty philosophy. In my day we worried about Vietnam. Hippies *cared* in those days.'

'Yes, I've heard your Bob Dylan records.'

'Do yourself a favour and get an education. I'll pay for it. At least know what you're dropping out *from*.'

'You think I don't?'

He had a sickening image of the new-look Dad fucking one of those empty snobbish girls across the bar. He left the cheque on the arm of his comfy pub armchair and lurched out into the street with a Guinness headache.

Paul actually feels too frail for the surf, he realises. He would never have imagined it but he is a shell, a piece of flotsam so insubstantial any one-footer could dump him. Even the neighbouring Hari Krishnas could have it all over him. Pallor, pony-tail top-knots and all, they are showing a joyous vigour and a surprisingly civilian ability at bodysurfing. In their flippers and Speedos they are just ordinary Aussie lads kicking on to the big ones, he thinks, struck abruptly by an idea for a painting, 'The Haris at Bondi', the three moon-white, scalped Haris frolicking among the suntans in the breakers. He has never painted this beach and would suddenly like the challenge. To get these mixed feelings down would be stimulating, the nice contrast of the hedonistic sun worshippers and the innocent eccentric sportsmen. Today, he notices, the beach has a post-impressionist, subjective atmosphere worth recording. There is a brightness defining the edges of the headlands and the roofs of the apartment blocks.

Excitement strikes Paul.

He is fidgety now with the idea of painting and gets up from the sand with surprising purpose to plot his creative plans. Ideas flit through his head. Trudging through the bustle of physical pleasure, the screams of children and the Gauguin fleshiness of bare-breasted women, he arrives unintentionally at the Bondi baths. Seeing further potential imaginative vistas in the green deep of the pool and its bordering white-painted rocks, he pays his entrance, takes off his T-shirt and dives in.

It's like swimming in the polar bears' pool at the zoo. The dark still water is overhung by rocks like simulated ice floes. He swims a length effortlessly and lightly, breathing freely in a new dream, turns and swims back, and then again, ten, twelve, sixteen times, half a mile.

Instead of bears the baths' other inhabitants are skylarking Maori children and elderly Middle Europeans playing cards. Paul spreads out to dry on the warm rocks among them. The sun beats on his eyelids; inside them a paramecium revolves. A blink and it changes pattern like a kaleidoscope. Someone touches his foot.

'I can't stand it, you following me around all the time,' announces Yvonne from Mario's café. Yvonne is wearing a black bikini bottom and a silver slave bracelet around one ankle. There are no paler marks where a bikini top could be. She is actually eating a Paddlepop, with aplomb, so symbolically he could laugh, her tongue never missing a drip, perched archly on the rocks with her high brown breasts pointing across the Pacific to New Zealand. They sit and talk. The surf breaks against the side of the baths. Sometimes a faint mist of spray passes over them. The tide turns; the sun over the apartment blocks creates half rainbows. Its brightness is refracted by the later hour and the humidity, the edges of the headlands are becoming softer too and the horizon is blurring.

While he's at it he could paint all this as well.

They leave together. There is hardly any conversation or indecision about their destination. Yvonne's flat is only two blocks away. It is small and its walls feature gift shop prints of big-eyed street waifs and sad anthropomorphic kittens. Paul blocks out the cats and waifs and more with a glass of wine and a shared joint. The lump is not in his mind to mention. His condition, he would have to say, is stable.

In bed Yvonne is lithe and passionate and full of grave and graceful tricks. She nibbles him with her little broken tooth and runs her tongue between his toes. She swivels around and over him, yelping, with her black hair in her eyes.

Paul licks the musky ear, feels the earrings with his teeth. He plunges into a South Seas heaven. He is totally submerged in thermal springs of heat and sweetness when he makes his final unfortunate discovery of the day. Through the front door and straight into the bedroom with amazing momentum arrives a

vision in pink and red, his flying head awhirl with wilting dread-
locks, his hands grabbing up anything for weapons, his sobbing
body a testament to instinct.

The Last Explorer

The last explorer wears green pyjamas, embossed with tiny heraldic shields, buttoned up to his chin. A pink coverlet is drawn up to his chest.

From his bed at the end of the ward he can see the Indian Ocean, choppy and blue, outside his window. He never learned to swim. The view of the sea is a favour they have given him, but he does not appreciate it.

Henry Ford also did not like the sea, a point he mentioned during their meeting in Detroit. Hence Ford's concentration on land transport.

The only 'ship' he himself appreciates is the 'ship of the desert' — the camel. The camel is the explorer's best friend, as long as you treat him fairly. You are mad to tease a camel. He can kill you by sitting on you. The chestbone takes the full weight of the camel's body when he squats. The chestbone is the camel's instrument of death.

He addressed the British on camels in 1933. The wireless station was in Hampstead. The publicity woman took him to lunch afterwards. The broadcast the British particularly lapped up was the one on the virtues of camels, especially their sense of humour. Camels like a joke. He told them about the camel which disgorged its entire half-digested meal over him, from head to waist, outside Tennant Creek. And that a camel never opens a gate, he just sits on it.

Miss Teasdale appreciated his camel anecdotes both during the broadcast and over lunch.

Funny, he told her, he'd used a motor for his first expedition in 1923, but after that he used camels. He switched to camels because they were slower. The slowness made them better for mineral surveying. In a motor you might ride right over something interesting without seeing it. Swaying along on a camel you could see a reef, some interesting feature, quite readily.

The wireless station played camel sound-effects from a gramophone record. The camel noises punctuating his talk included bells, bazaar bartering and guttural exclamations in Arabic. Miss Teasdale said the British listening public wouldn't know the difference.

The last explorer's body makes hardly a lump under the covers. Against a pile of pillows his big pale, strong-jawed head seems disembodied. He removes a hand from under the bedclothes to slowly rub his eyes. They overdid the sleeping drug again last night.

It is awkward being here.

He thought he would be out of here within twenty-four hours.

He has twenty-three lines in *Who's Who*. 'Explorer, broadcaster, author, Fellow of the Royal Geographical Society . . .' A life of luck and action encapsulated in a paragraph. He wore a Colt .38 on his belt. He forbade his white men to take their revolvers off their gunbelts. Better safe than sorry.

In London both times he wore a double-breasted suit and his Royal Navy Air Service tie from fighting with the White Russians against the Reds in 1917. He cut a dash.

He was popular with the Fleet Street boys with his demonstration of Aboriginal sign language and how to make fires in Hampstead with sticks. Miss Teasdale kindly arranged the photographic sessions and afterwards they went off to the Dorchester and discussed the desert.

She asked enthusiastic questions about risks and deprivation. An understanding of man's inner resources was not beyond her.

Grace would not face the desert.

Grace desired the coast; it was a mistake. A house facing the sea, looking back towards England, was her wish. She refused to turn her back on the coast.

The house on the hill at Cottesloe was always windy because she had to face the ocean. For five years the sea-breeze howled through the pines and slammed the doors. A small dugite crawled across the lawn from the golf links. While Grace swooned on the buffalo grass he cracked its back like a whip.

Captain Scott-Bowdler was never optimistic about their chances. He couldn't visualise his daughter as a West Australian. Night after night Grace sat on the verandah facing the ocean and writing letters home.

On one expedition he rode camels from Alice Springs to Laverton on a nine-month nickel survey. He had his affinity for the desert and two good men under him. Purposely they travelled slowly and allowed themselves to get three months behind, spinning out their rations with bush tucker. They relied on themselves and their bushcraft. When they finally reached Laverton they circled the town on their camels for two days. They didn't want to come in.

Grace was not sitting on the verandah, she was two months gone on the *Stratheden*. The opal he found for her at Lightning Ridge was on the dresser with her front door key.

There was a shipping list cut from the *West Australian* with the *Stratheden*'s departure time circled. The cutting was yellow by then and the *Stratheden* well and truly berthed and unloaded at Southampton.

It was the old *Oakland* he caught to San Francisco, then the train from Oakland to Detroit via Chicago.

It was true what they said about Henry Ford being as tight as a fish's rectum.

Ford gave him coffee and one fig newton and listened intently to his tale. He said, 'You're a very fine and ambitious young man,' shook his hand again and kept his wallet in his pocket.

So he travelled on to Washington and sold his photographs and story to the National Geographic Society for $150, big money in those days.

The Royal Geographic Society was also generous in spirit. In London they gave a special dinner for him, the youngest man ever to read a paper to the Society, and Captain Scott-Bowdler introduced him to Grace. This was after his first expedition when he crossed the continent from east to west, three thousand miles from Winton, Queensland, to Broome, Western Australia.

For transport he chose a ten-year-old Model-T Ford which cost him £50. Because of the climate and terrain he replaced its wooden wheels with metal ones. He put in a magneto because the coils were dodgy. He met a man in a pub with £4/1/3 and made him an expedition partner. They crossed the desert on £8/13/2 and arrived in Broome ten months later, where he sold the Ford for £100.

His epic trip would surely earn him a fortune from the Ford Company. He travelled to America and gained an audience with the founder. He had a manila folder containing suggestions for advertising and promotion and his fig newton vanished in one eager bite.

Henry Ford was more in awe of his sea trip across the Pacific. He still had the *Titanic* on the brain.

As for the Model-T crossing the Australian desert, east to west, Ford said that was only to be expected. It was a Ford after all.

* * *

Recovery from a cerebral haemorrhage is slow at eighty-two, he must be realistic. He has been thinking again that there is something behind his existence. It was obviously planned for him to do things.

In the Depression men were in a mess and had confidence in him. In the thirties he was never busier or more prosperous. He'd return from some expedition or other thinking 'that's that' and next week he'd be out again on the camels from Darwin to Adelaide, from Port Hedland to Melbourne.

For twenty years he led expeditions into the interior on behalf of companies seeking minerals. He surveyed geographical and geological features, made botanical, soil and meteorological readings, assayed deposits, discovered new lakes and rare caves and took photographs by the thousand.

He mapped a lot of country.

Moira Teasdale enjoyed his story about crouching behind a barricade of camel saddles while he fought off hostile blacks. At the Dorchester he ate asparagus and a chicken-and-leek pie and she said it was better than Kipling to listen to him.

The blacks crept up on their camp in their feathered *kadaitcha* boots to spear them. Luckily Tommy the camel boy, camped thirty yards away, spotted them. They got behind the saddles and fought them off all night.

Moira's letter caught up with him in Wyndham. Her face today is a blur but Grace's is clear. Occasionally in dreams they run together. Scott-Bowdler said marrying an Australian was a curious thing. Maybe so, maybe less curious than sitting on a verandah staring at the Indian Ocean.

The explorer's life is an independent one. He never got around to replying. In the desert he attempted three letters but threw them away. Another English woman, what was the point? At the time he was recovering from another snake bite, a gwarder, and not himself. The venom confuses you.

The next night the blacks returned. But I scared them away for good. To be frank, Miss Teasdale, they ran away because in all the ruddy panic I got tangled up in my mosquito net. I stood up like a white ghost and they fled into the spinifex.

I thought you'd enjoy that story.

In the early morning when he is lying there, the only patient awake, the sea shallows are dotted with variously coloured balls or buoys. Against his will he looked, turned away and they were gone. A nurse had no answer to his question. Not for some time did it dawn on him they were women's bathing caps.

Women were bobbing in the waves in the early morning, chatting to each other.

The penny dropped when he saw them walking up the hill from the beach into the pines, most of them elderly and wearing bathing gowns over their swimming costumes. A couple of them still had their bathing caps on.

As soon as his curiosity was satisfied he again lost all interest in the sea.

Unless he is drugged he does not sleep. He lives on air, he hardly moves. He has been made aware of the salivation problem and keeps a handkerchief handy for the dribble.

Strange tastes come into his mouth. Once it was damper, burnt and crunchy. Once it was grilled barramundi. Another time sour-grass. In dreams caused by sleeping pills he sometimes smells camels' breath and feels his nostrils clogged with dust.

A Fleet Street interviewer asked him in 1933 what the desert meant to him. The question stopped him in his tracks. 'Finding your own love,' he remembers replying. Moira touched his sleeve. It still embarrasses him to recall saying it.

He runs his book titles through his mind. There were six books but today he can remember only four, all out of print. They were all most discursive on exploration.

The National Library has all his expeditions' logbooks and the thousands of photographs taken over the years. Sand fell from the spines of his logbooks when he plonked them on the Chief Librarian's desk.

His life and expeditions are now in the hands of the general public.

In his papers for the library he found a social page from a 1924 edition of the London *Daily Telegraph* recording the marriage.

He came up the steps. There were pine cones on the verandah, blown there by the sea breeze. The opal was on the dresser and the shipping list.

He was lucky to be out of it.

He was known for his many lucky escapes. He always knew the right people. He was good in a crisis, the men put their trust in him. He showed the Fleet Street boys how to make fire in Hampstead with sticks. Never tease a camel, he advised the British.

When we got to the town we circled it on our camels. We didn't want to come in.

A young woman approaches his bed. Her skin is sun-tanned, she has a bossy, confident manner.

'Have we done a wee this morning?' she demands.

He stares past her. His face is white as paper.

'Yes,' says the last explorer.

When she is gone he lies back on his pillows with the heavy pulse of the sea and the whine of the sea-breeze in his ears.

A little later he manages to slowly remove the bedclothes. He inches himself out of bed. Supporting himself on the head rail, he

154

carefully stands. He holds on to the head rail of the bed and pushes. The bed moves silently on its coasters.

He manages to turn the bed completely around. With difficulty he climbs back into bed. His pulse is racing. Gradually he relaxes and lies back on his pillows, staring into the far distance. He cannot see out the window. The sea is behind his back, its noise is gone.

Facing the desert, he feels up to laughing.

Stingray

Something miraculous happens, thinks David, when you dive into the surf at Bondi after a bad summer's day. Today had been humid and grim, full of sticky tension since this morning when he'd spilled black coffee down the crotch of his new Italian cotton suit. He'd had professional and private troubles, general malaise and misery pounding behind his eyes as he drove home to his flat. He was still bruised from his marriage dissolution, abraded from the ending of a love affair and all the way up William Street the car radio news had elaborated on a pop star's heroin and tequila overdose. Then in New South Head Road it warned that child prostitution was rife and economic depression imminent. Markets tumbled and kids sold themselves. Only the coffee stain on his trousers and his awareness of his own body smell prevented him from stopping at the Lord Dudley and sinking many drinks. Instead, a mild brainwave struck him — he'd have a swim.

The electric cleansing of the surf is astonishing, the cold effervescing over the head and trunk and limbs. And the internal results are a greater wonder. At once the spirits lift. There is a grateful pleasure in the last hour of softer December daylight. The brain sharpens. The body is charged with agility and grubby lethargy swept away.

David swims vigorously beyond the breakers until he is the farthest swimmer out. He feels he could swim forever. He swims onto a big wave, surfs it to the beach. In the crystal evening ocean he even gambols. He is anticipating another arched wave, striking out before it through a small patch of floating weed, when there is an explosion of pain in his right hand.

David stands in chest-deep water shaking his hand in surprise. He's half-aware of a creature camouflaged in the weed scraps and wavelets, on the defensive and aimed at his chest. As he flails away from it into clear water it vanishes. Immediately it seems as if it had never existed and that his demonstration of stunned agony is an affectation, like the exaggerated protestations of a child. But the hand he holds out of the sea is bleeding freely from the little finger and swelling even as he stumbles ashore.

Pain speeds quickly to deeper levels, and then expands. Bleeding from a small jagged hole between the joints, the finger balloons to the size of a thumb, then to a taut, blotchy sausage. Even so, the pain is out of proportion to the minor nature of the wound. This sensation belongs to a bloody, heaving stump. Dripping water and blood, David trudges up the beach, up the steps of the bathing pavilion, to the first-aid room, where the beach inspector washes and nonchalantly probes the wound with a lancet. 'Lots of sting-rays out there at the moment,' he volunteers.

The point of the knife seems to touch a nerve. It's all he can do not to cry out. 'Is that what it was?' he asks. His voice sounds like someone speaking on the telephone, mechanical and breathless. The beach inspector shrugs. 'I can't find any spine in it.' He gives a final jab of the lancet to make sure.

'Shouldn't you warn the swimmers?' David suggests, making a conscious effort to sound normal. He wants to see signs erected, warning whistles blown. He's beginning to shiver and notices that he has covered the floor of the beach inspector's room with sand and water and a dozen or so drops of blood. He feels ruffled and awry; glancing down he sees one of his balls has come out of his bathers in the panic; he adjusts himself with his good hand.

The beach inspector is dabbing mercurichrome on his wounded finger. On *his* hand a blue tattooed shark swims sinuously among the wrist hairs and veins. He shrugs again. 'Stingrays're pretty shy unless you tread on them.'

'Not so shy!'

The beach inspector screws the top back on his mercurichrome bottle. 'I'd get up to the hospital if I were you,' he suggests laconically. 'You never know.'

By instinct David drives home, left-handed, his pulsating right hand hooked over the wheel. Impossibly, the pain worsens. In Bondi Road he is struck by the word POISON. He is poisoned. This country is world champion in the venomous creatures' department. The box jellyfish. Funnel-web spiders. Stonefish. The tiny blue-ringed octopus, carrying enough venom to paralyse ten grown men. The land and sea abound with evil stingers. It suddenly occurs to him he might be about to die. The randomness and lack of moment are right. Venom is coursing through his body. Stopped at the Bondi Road and Oxford Street lights, he waits in the car for progressive paralysis. Is it the breathing or the heart that stops? In the evening traffic he is scared but oddly calm, to the extent of noting the strong smell of frangipani in Edgecliff Road. He knows that trivia fills the mind at the end: his mother's last words to him were, 'Your baked beans are on the stove.' Baked beans and frangipani scent, not exactly grave and pivotal last thoughts.

It would be ironic for such a beach lover to die from the sea. David has known people killed by the sea, three or four, drowned mostly in yachting accidents over the years. He certainly has a respectful attitude to the sea — as a young lifesaver he even saved a handful of drowning swimmers himself. Thinking back, he has never heard of anyone dying from a stingray sting, unless the shock touched off a cardiac arrest. This knowledge gives small comfort as a new spasm of pain shoots up his arm.

He gets the car home, parks loosely against the kerb and carries his hand inside. He circles the small living room holding his hand. Left-handed, he pours himself a brandy and drinks a mouthful, then, wondering whether it is wise to mix poison and alcohol, pours the brandy down the sink. The hand throbs now with a power all its own and the agitation it causes prevents him even from sitting down. The hand dominates the room; it seems to fill the whole flat. He wishes to relinquish responsibility for it as he has done for much of his past life.

Living alone suddenly acquires a new meaning. Expiring privately on the beige living-room carpet from a stingray sting would be too conducive to mordant dinner-party wit. He considers phoning Angela, his former wife. He imagines himself announcing, 'Sorry to bother you. A stingray stung me,' and her turning to her new friend Gordon, a hand over the mouthpiece, their gins and tonics arrested, saying, 'Now he's been stung by a stingray!' (He never could leave well enough alone.)

She would hurry over, of course. She was cool in a crisis. Gordon would hold the fort. Gordon was adept at holding the fort, perhaps because it wasn't Gordon's fort. This did not stop Gordon from making proprietorial gestures, sitting him down in his old chair and pouring him convivial drinks in his old glasses, when he dropped the children off.

'He's wonderful with the kids,' she'd said, driving a barb into David's heart.

He doesn't phone.

He is becoming distracted and decides to telephone Victoria, of whom he is fond. She has mentioned recently at lunch that her present relationship is in its terminal stage and he feels that a stingray mercy dash may not be beyond her.

'Christ Almighty,' she says. 'Don't move. Sit down or something.' In ten minutes she is running up his stairs, panicking at the door with tousled hair and no make-up, and ushering him into her Volkswagen.

The casualty ward at St Vincent's is crowded with victims of the city summer night. Lacerated drunks rant along the corridors. Young addicts are rushed in, comatose, attached to oxygen. Under questioning, pale concussees try to guess what day it is and count backwards from one hundred.

'Please don't wait around for me,' David tells Victoria, painfully filling in forms about next of kin. He can barely print. He can't remember his brother Max's address.

'I'll wait,' she insists.

As he and his hand are led into the hospital's inner recesses he glances back at Victoria, rumpled and out of kilter, perched on the edge of a waiting-room chair. Their parting seems suddenly quietly dramatic, moving, curiously cinematic. From beneath her ruffled spaniel's hairstyle she smiles anxiously, reflecting this telepathic mood. Rubberised black curtains close behind him.

Among the sea of street and household injuries David's finger is a medical curiosity. A young Malaysian doctor with acned cheeks informs him, 'We'll play it by the book.' Self-consciously squatting on a narrow bed in an open cubicle, his shoulder blades and buttocks exposed traditionally in a green hospital gown, David is not necessarily relieved.

It was never him in hospitals. It was usually women — having babies, miscarriages, assorted gynaecological conditions which owed something to his participation. They always wanted him present. Alone with his unique sting he understands. He lies back holding his own hand.

They innoculate him against tetanus, take his blood pressure, pulse and temperature readings and a urine sample. They wash and dress the finger and apply a bandage tourniquet to his forearm. 'We

162

want to keep an eye on you,' says the Malaysian doctor. Around his cubicle the raving of grazed drunks continues. He hears a nurse's voice say, 'It's no use, we'll have to put the straps on.' A man howls often and mournfully for 'Nora'. In answer to a nurse's shouted question a concussed woman suggests it is the month of August.

'Close,' says the nurse.

'March?' says the woman.

David calls for a nurse and asks whether Victoria is still in the waiting room. 'Please tell her to go home.' A moment later she peers through his curtains, enters, sits on the edge of the bed and holds his good hand.

'You look vulnerable,' she tells him, touching his bare back.

'So do you, actually.'

'I came out in a hurry.'

Amid some commotion four medical staff now wheel an unconscious young woman into the cubicle in front. The staff try to bring her round but the girl, dark-haired and with even, small features, seems to be fighting consciousness. All at once she threshes and moans and tosses her naked body against its restraining straps. 'Hilary! Hilary!' the nurses shout. 'Come on, Hilary. Be a good girl!'

'What are you still doing here?' David asks Victoria. 'It's getting late.'

'I want to wait.'

'I'm all right. I'm under observation.'

'Do shut up.'

Hilary is given the stomach-pump. The staff attach her to oxygen and various intravenous drips, all the time yelling and laughing in strained cameraderie. Hilary is one of them, their age. Immediately David sees Helena in five, ten years time, her straight hair, her suddenly longer, womanly limbs, her emotional problems. His pulse beneath the tourniquet throbs almost audibly. 'Hilary! Hilary! Do you know where you are?' the nurses sing. His fault.

He and Victoria are silent in sight of this drama. Though the pain doesn't let up he thinks he is getting used to it and feels slightly ridiculous being here.

'Nora, I want Nora,' howls the man.

David wants nothing more at this instant than for Hilary to recover.

A violent commotion comes from the girl's cubicle. Suddenly it is jammed with doctors, nurses and orderlies. The Malaysian doctor is wrestling her, so are two sisters and a nurse. Everyone is loudly swearing and grunting, her bed is shaking, metal clangs and instruments fall to the floor.

'God!' cries David.

They are forcing something down Hilary's throat and mixed up in her gagging and moaning is a cry of outrage and ferocity.

Victoria's hand is squeezing his good one with great pressure. The howling man is muffled by the tumult from the cubicle opposite, now jammed with what seems like the complete hospital staff. Hilary begins to gag again, vomits, and all the staff exclaim and curse angrily. Then they start to laugh. They are all covered in black liquid, the emetic they had forced into her stomach. Hilary has vomited up her pills.

At 2.00 a.m. they release him. Victoria drives him home and keeps him under observation for the rest of the night.

Though the pain lessens next day, six months later the tip of his finger is still numb, the nerve-endings damaged. Victoria, early in their living together, produces one evening a copy of *Venomous Creatures of Australia*, reading which it becomes clear to David that his attacker was most likely a butterfly cod, a small brown fish which looks like a weed.

164

'They're actually very poisonous,' she says generously. 'People are thought to have died.'

'Let's keep it a stingray,' he says.